HARLEQUIN

MEDICAL
ROMANCE

Falling Again in El Salvador

JULIE DANVERS

LARGER PRINT

ISBN-13: 978-1-335-40427-5

As the rider pulled up beside her, his half-shaven face hidden by splattered mud and thick goggles, she allowed herself a moment to appreciate the aesthetics of such a beautiful machine.

The body was powerfully built, gracefully compact and radiating an almost-magnetic heat.

The bike was nice, too.

The rider simply sat next to her for a moment. Cassie felt as though he were staring, but she couldn't read his expression—the goggles completely covered his eyes. Then he cut the engine and eased his body off his motorcycle. He was six feet of lean, angular muscle. He wore a leather bomber jacket and jeans that hugged his thighs. A shock of brown hair flopped over his forehead, which he pushed up as he lifted the goggles to the crown of his head, revealing deep-set brown eyes. They were eyes Cassie recognized: pools of tenderness in an angular face.

Eyes she hadn't seen in five years. Not since her surgical rotation. Eyes that belonged to…

"Bryce?" she said. She wasn't prepared for the well of emotion that sprang to her voice.

"Hey, Cass," he said. "Sorry I'm late."

Dear Reader,

I'm a huge believer in second chances. I honestly don't know where I'd be without them. As a writer and as a human being, there are so many times when I've been grateful to have a second chance... or a third...or a twentieth. Somehow, even the things we know intimately can look different with a fresh start.

Cassie Andover is certainly hoping for a fresh start when she joins Medicine International in El Salvador. But the minute she begins her new job, she's met by Bryce Hamlin, an old flame she hasn't seen in five years. Cassie can't help noticing that Bryce has changed. The cautious man she once knew is now tearing through the jungle on a motorcycle and delivering medical supplies via helicopter. Cassie and Bryce have a complicated past...but if they can start over, they just might have a beautiful future.

Falling Again in El Salvador includes so much of what I love about medical romance. Writing this book brought some much-needed excitement into my life, and I hope it will for you, too. Stop by my website, juliedanvers.wordpress.com, and let me know! And you're welcome to follow me on Twitter @_juliedanvers.

Warmly,

Julie Danvers

FALLING AGAIN IN EL SALVADOR

JULIE DANVERS

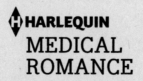

HARLEQUIN

MEDICAL
ROMANCE

H HARLEQUIN®
MEDICAL
ROMANCE™

Recycling programs
for this product may
not exist in your area.

ISBN-13: 978-1-335-40427-5

Falling Again in El Salvador

Copyright © 2020 by Alexis Silas

This edition published by arrangement with Harlequin Books S.A.

For questions and comments about the quality of this book, please contact us at CustomerService@Harlequin.com.

Harlequin Enterprises ULC
22 Adelaide St. West, 40th Floor
Toronto, Ontario M5H 4E3, Canada
www.Harlequin.com

Printed in U.S.A.

Julie Danvers grew up in a rural community surrounded by farmland. Although her town was small, it offered plenty of scope for imagination, as well as an excellent library. Books allowed Julie to have many adventures from her own home, and her love affair with reading has never ended. She loves to write about heroes and heroines who are adventurous, passionate about a cause, and looking for the best in themselves and others. Julie's website is juliedanvers.wordpress.com.

Books by Julie Danvers

Harlequin Medical Romance

From Hawaii to Forever

Visit the Author Profile page at Harlequin.com.

To my best friend, foxhole buddy
and partner in crime.

CHAPTER ONE

CASSIE ANDOVER HAD been waiting at the Miraflores bus stop for almost two hours before she decided that her ride was not going to show up.

She was on the last leg of an increasingly arduous journey. After a tearful goodbye to her parents at the airport in Manhattan, she'd rushed to make her flight to El Salvador, only to learn that it had been delayed. By the time she arrived in the capital city of San Salvador, she'd missed the first bus to Miraflores, and the second was so crowded that the driver wouldn't allow her to bring her overstuffed hiking backpack on board. The third bus had been blessedly empty, and she'd dozed off for most of the ride, only waking when the bus jerked to a halt.

Now, as she felt the sudden jolt of the bus stopping, she blinked her sleepy eyes open. The bus window revealed a landscape of lush green coffee fields over rolling hills. In the distance, she could see mountains wreathed with blue haze…and nothing else. No buildings, no sign of a town and no other people.

The driver swung the bus door open and waited. When Cassie made no motion to move, he said, "Miraflores," expectantly.

"But that can't be," Cassie said. Six months ago, when she'd accepted her new job as an obstetrician with Medicine International, she'd started intensive refresher courses to improve her Spanish. Her preparation served her well now as she argued with the bus driver that this could not possibly be Miraflores.

"Miraflores is supposed to be a small town," she said. "There's no town here. There's nothing. There's barely even a road."

"Miraflores *is* a small town," the driver replied. "But this is the *bus stop* for Miraflores. You want to go to Miraflores itself, you'll need to walk two miles east or find a ride."

Cassie looked at the patch of grass the driver had referred to as a bus stop. There was a knee-high concrete stump that seemed to be a road marker, but otherwise the dirt road that stretched into the distance appeared no different than it had for the past fifty miles.

"You're sure this is the right bus stop?" she asked again. "If someone said they would meet me at the Miraflores bus stop, then this would be the place?"

"It's the only Miraflores bus stop that I know about," the driver said. "You're welcome to stay on board, but I won't be stopping again until we get to San Alejo."

Cassie glanced at her phone. No bars. She might be able to make a call from San Alejo, but that would mean several more hours on the bus, and after a full day of traveling, she needed a rest. Even if that meant sitting by the side of an unknown road in the middle of nowhere.

She wrestled her giant backpack off the bus and settled down to wait as the driver left in a cloud of dust.

The sky was clear, and the air was still and quiet, punctuated by occasional notes of birdsong. The road ran along a hill, which deepened into a valley below, revealing coffee fields that stretched all the way to the mountains on the horizon. To the right of the road, tall ferns quickly thickened into a deep tropical forest.

Aside from the neat green rows of the coffee fields, Cassie could see no other signs of civilization. She was completely, utterly alone.

Well, almost alone. A single chicken emerged

from the thick jungle foliage, pecking its way through the grass at the roadside.

You wanted to get away from New York, Cassie reminded herself. *You wanted to reconnect with what really mattered to you. Now that it's just you and the chickens, maybe you'll get your chance.*

Cassie had come to El Salvador in desperate need of a change. Being known as the best ob-gyn in New York City came at a price, and years of meeting the demands of New York's society mothers had left Cassie feeling burned-out and disillusioned with medicine.

She'd never imagined that delivering babies could lead to burnout. Cassie had been born with a congenital heart defect, and it meant the world to her to be able to provide infants and mothers with the care they needed, just as Cassie and her family had needed extra care when she was born. But as Cassie's reputation as an obstetrician had grown, her career had taken an unexpected turn, and she found herself increasingly in demand with New York's wealthiest and most well-known families. When she'd started her job, it wasn't unusual for patients to make special requests for mood music and underwater births, but it had become increasingly common for mothers to welcome their infants into the world with live string quartets, and the pools for the underwater births were filled with expensive water filtered through volcanic rock. Cassie's clientele wanted designer maternity care, and the mothers she worked with were not shy about voicing their displeasure when their demands couldn't be met.

"I feel like I don't know who I am anymore," she'd told her best friend, Vanessa, a fellow obstetrician. "All I do is run myself ragged while my patients complain that the walnuts in their macrobiotic salad are unevenly chopped, or that the lactation consultant can't figure out their custom-fitted Louis Vuitton breast pump."

"That's what you get for being the best," Vanessa had replied. "When you're providing maternity care for the wealthy, they think they can have anything as long as they can pay for it. Last week I had a senator's wife yell at me for thirty minutes because I refused to give her baby his first bath using San Pellegrino sparkling water—she got the idea from that pop star who had twins a few months ago. She said I'd be hearing from her if her kid didn't get into Collegiate."

Cassie shook her head. "I always thought that by the time I turned thirty, I'd have a relationship I cared about and a career that meant something to me. But now I wonder if I'm even supposed to be a doctor."

"Maybe you just need a change," Vanessa had proposed. "We get so much pressure from hospital administration to cater to the whims of wealthier patients. Instead of focusing on medicine, we're forced to meet the demands of parents who are acting like babies themselves. That's why you don't feel like yourself anymore—you're not connecting with what really matters to you about medicine. Maybe you just need to work in a different setting."

Vanessa's words had haunted Cassie for weeks. She had to admit that her heart leaped at the idea of leaving Brooklyn General Hospital for something…*more*. The trouble was, she wasn't sure what *something more* might be. She had a steady, secure job at a hospital with the best obstetrics department in the city. If this wasn't the right setting for her, then what was?

Her job at Brooklyn General was safe and dependable. It made no sense to leave. And she might have stayed there forever, if she hadn't been offered the promotion.

They'd asked her to be the head of Brooklyn General's Obstetrics Department. But just before she agreed, a vision of the next ten years flashed before Cassie's eyes. Longer shifts at the hospital, with fewer days off. Endless deliveries of babies born with a higher net worth than she had in student loans. Hours spent soothing the feelings of new parents not because they were afraid or in distress but because their decaf no-foam latte lacked the exact amount of cinnamon they'd requested. Explaining to mothers that they didn't have to keep the placenta and that no matter *what* the latest internet celebrity had done with hers, it was probably against all medical advice.

As Cassie envisioned her future at the hospital, she couldn't deny the sinking feeling in her stomach. Or that nagging little voice in her mind, the one that reminded her of how her heart had soared at the idea of something *more*. That voice wasn't so little anymore. In fact, it was louder than ever.

Her lips had parted to say "yes" to her safe, predictable future…but the words that had come out instead were, "I quit."

She'd used her new abundance of free time to research options for doctors who wanted to work abroad, and she learned about Medicine International, a relief organization that placed health-care professionals into community agencies around the world. They had a need for good obstetricians.

Six months later, she found herself sitting on an unknown road in El Salvador with only a chicken for company. Wondering what she'd gotten herself into.

It had been a long time since Cassie had taken such a risk. Growing up with a heart defect meant that she'd spent her childhood surrounded by well-meaning adults who wanted to protect her. Her parents were constantly telling her to slow down and be more careful, even when she'd wanted to do things as commonplace as playing tag or riding bicycles with other children.

She knew that her parents had good reason to be overprotective, but she couldn't help chafing against all of the rules and restrictions that governed her life. The result was a serious daredevil phase by the time she entered medical school. Her heart was finally as healthy as anyone else's, and for the first time in her life, she was determined to live without fear. In pursuit of this goal, she threw herself into every daring activity she could think of. She bought a motorcycle and explored the countryside surrounding New York. She took a class on rock climbing and rappelling, loving the thrill of pushing off from high places. She visited karaoke bars and belted out terrible songs at the top of her lungs.

She also started dating the surgical resident supervising her clinical rotation.

Residents and medical students weren't supposed to date, but Cassie was fed up with rules. For the first time, she was following what was in her heart rather than obsessing over how to protect it. And it was glorious… right up until she made a terrible mistake.

Her professors had always praised her ability to make quick, bold decisions in clinical situations. A bright and gifted medical student, heady with freedom and confidence for the first time in her life, Cassie never hesitated to argue a point if she believed she was right.

And she'd believed she was right that night to push the surgical team into taking a risk with a patient. She may not have been responsible for the final judgment call—that had been the chief resident's decision—but she was certain that if she hadn't pushed, if she hadn't convinced him to take action, that he would not have made such a risky decision.

Then again, maybe if they hadn't been in a relationship, he simply would have pulled rank and ignored her protests.

And then maybe none of the heartbreak that followed would have happened.

Even though the patient survived, they both

faced disciplinary action. He was put on probation and denied a competitive fellowship he'd applied for, while she received nothing more than a stern dressing down from the hospital's training committee. It still made her cheeks burn to think how lightly she'd gotten off, while someone else suffered for her reckless behavior.

Riddled with guilt, she'd broken things off with him. She'd already put his job at risk and cost him a prestigious fellowship. If anyone found out they were dating, it would be the last straw for him. She couldn't cause any more disruption to his life.

She left him a note, trying and failing to put all she felt into words. She felt a little guilty about sneaking off into the dead of night, but she knew that if she faced him, she'd never be able to go through with the breakup. And she had to go through with the breakup. She could handle her own heartbreak, but she couldn't handle the thought of causing a good man even more pain than she already had.

She took a leave of absence from medical school, and returned home to live with her parents for a while. She resumed her clinical training the next fall. And while she still couldn't let go of her guilt, she could at least vow to be more cautious and careful.

It wasn't difficult to keep that vow. She was at a new hospital, and everyone she'd known had moved on with their lives…including, apparently, the young surgeon she'd fallen for. There was no sign of him anywhere in the New York medical community, and Cassie was determined not to look for him. She'd broken the rules by dating him in the first place. He was part of a reckless phase in her past that she intended to leave behind.

It was the best way to ensure that no one else got hurt, in her love life or in her professional career. She threw herself into her work, devoting herself to her job and to her patients. Instead of going rock climbing and singing at karaoke bars, she worked twelve-hour shifts at the hospital. Her colleagues noticed her dedication and admired her for it, but she never felt she deserved their recognition. She'd only begun working so hard in the first place in order to repair her reputation after making a huge mistake. Nevertheless, her hard work paid off. Five years later, she was the most in demand ob-gyn in New York.

She was successful, respected in her field… and very much alone.

As she let work take over more of her life,

she had less time for the things she enjoyed. But that craving for something *more* still nagged at the back of her mind, no matter how often she tried to swat it away.

She was certain that if she had accepted the promotion and stayed in New York, she would have said goodbye to her adventurous side forever. Instead, for the first time since medical school, she'd decided to take a risk. And this time, she was determined to make the most of it. Without anyone else getting hurt.

Now, as she gazed at the mountain in the distance, she couldn't help feeling a thrill, despite her fatigue. She'd read that El Salvador was one of the most beautiful—and dangerous—countries in the world. She could see that everything she'd read and heard about El Salvador's beauty held true, and she could already feel the part of her that craved excitement coming alive again.

But before Cassie could find her adventurous side, she needed to find a way to get to the medical outpost. She frowned at the sun, which was beginning to dip lower toward the horizon.

Where the hell was her ride?

She stood up from the road marker she'd been leaning against and gave her arms an experimental flex. Resting by the road had done her good after so much travel, but she needed to get moving. It was one thing to be enchanted by the thought of rain forests, rugged terrain and wildlife during the daytime, but Cassie didn't relish the idea of waiting out in the open after nightfall.

Her monolithic backpack loomed beside her. She felt a twinge of longing for her motorcycle, which she'd had to sell before leaving New York. Not that she'd ever made time to ride. Her Kawasaki Z650 had sat neglected in a garage while Cassie worked sixty-hour weeks at the hospital.

You wanted to get back to basics, she reminded herself.

And now you're getting what you asked for. At least it's just a two-mile hike. With aching muscles and a touch of sleep deprivation. While carrying a giant backpack that contains all your worldly possessions.

With a sigh, she eased the backpack onto her shoulders and began to hike down the road toward Miraflores.

Bryce Hamlin could see that the baby was breech.

He'd suspected as much. He'd been monitoring Mrs. Martinez's pregnancy closely ever since she'd arrived at the medical outpost several months ago with her family, all of whom had been suffering from malaria. Mr. Martinez had not survived. Mrs. Martinez and her ten-year-old son, Manuel, had recovered, but she had been six-months pregnant at the time and Bryce knew that a hard pregnancy could often mean a dangerous birth.

So he wasn't entirely surprised when the camp medical director, Enrique Garcia, told him that Mrs. Martinez had gone into labor and that the midwife needed his help. Enrique had stopped Bryce just as he was readying his motorcycle for the trip through the rain forest to pick up the new obstetrician, who should be waiting at the Miraflores bus stop and who was probably already wondering where he was.

As Bryce came into the main birthing tent, one of the midwives, Anna, met him with a nod. "We're having a rough start," she said. "She's fully dilated, but labor isn't progressing. I'm still not certain about a natural birth. A C-section could help to avoid complications."

Bryce nodded. A C-section might be necessary, but he wanted to avoid one if at all possible. Without the luxury of equipment such as ultrasound machines or fetal heart monitors, a cesarean birth could create as many risks as it prevented.

Right on cue, a faint, almost imperceptible tremor flared across his hands, reminding him that a lack of modern medical equipment wasn't the only risk factor. He forced himself to ignore the tremor and focused on assessing the position of the baby's head and back. He placed his hands on Mrs. Martinez's abdomen, relieved that she seemed to feel calm.

"You couldn't just wait for me to get back with the new obstetrician, could you, Mrs. Martinez?" he teased.

She smiled back at him. "You've taken such good care of my family since we arrived here. I guess this little one wants you as its doctor, too."

It was all too easy to feel the baby's position through Mrs. Martinez's thin skin: a frank breech position, the baby was ready to make its way into the world buttocks-first. He was needed here. The new doctor, whoever they were, would just have to wait a little longer.

"We'll try a little longer for a natural delivery," he told Anna and Mrs. Martinez. "But let's all be ready in case we have to do a C-section."

As Mrs. Martinez pushed with each contraction, Bryce patiently waited for the baby's bottom half to emerge. Anna stood at Mrs. Martinez's head, glancing worriedly at Bryce from time to time, but Bryce continued to wait, letting Mrs. Martinez and the baby do most of the work. Despite the risks involved in a breech birth, he knew the baby's best chances lay in practicing immense patience at the start of labor, even when every instinct clamored for him to *do* something. In this baby's case, the best thing he could do was wait.

His trust was rewarded as the baby's hindquarters slowly began to emerge. Bryce gently pulled out the baby's legs and grabbed the towel that Anna handed him.

"It's a girl," Anna whispered to Mrs. Martinez, whose face was a mix of pain, joy and exhaustion.

Bryce wrapped the towel around the baby's body and began to pull gently along with the contractions, first helping the baby's left shoulder be born, then the entire left arm.

Now for the tricky part.

He slowly rotated the baby in a 180-degree circle. With the baby still facing downward, he felt for the baby's cheekbones with his fingers. There—he could just rest his fingers on the baby's cheeks for leverage.

Bryce nodded at Anna. "Now," he said.

Anna placed her hand on Mrs. Martinez's abdomen and pressed down while Bryce pulled, and suddenly a procedure that had been happening very slowly became very fast—the baby's head shot out into the world, Bryce found himself holding a very slippery and squirmy bundle and the baby filled her lungs and gave a full-throated cry, announcing her arrival.

Now for the best part.

Bryce swaddled the baby in the towel he'd used to deliver her and placed her in Mrs. Martinez's waiting arms. It was a sight that never got old—a new life coming into the world, a parent gazing into a newborn's eyes for the first time.

"Congratulations, Mrs. Martinez," he said. "You both did great."

Mrs. Martinez was able to spare him a quick glance and a smile before she turned her gaze back to the bundle in her arms. "I'm so glad you were here, Doctor," she said, though her expression was wholly absorbed in the little one she held. "I knew we were never in any danger the whole time."

Bryce's hands twitched. He'd lost track of time during the labor, and the tremor in his hands was always worse when he was fatigued.

"I'll let you two get to know each other," he said, and stepped outside the birthing tent.

Outside, Bryce sat beneath a sturdy balsa tree and leaned his back against the trunk. He let out a long slow breath. His hands, the traitors, had stopped their trembling. They hardly ever shook now, but the tremors had a way of flaring up at the worst possible moments. He flexed and stretched his fingers. Taking a few minutes to calm himself before and after a procedure always helped to settle things down.

Years ago, Bryce had been a talented surgeon, just one month away from completing his residency. He'd always dreamed of becoming a neurosurgeon, performing operations on the brain and spinal cord. But with one wild swerve from a drunk driver on a highway, his life was changed forever. After the accident, hundreds of hours of physical therapy had allowed him to regain much of the control and flexibility in his fingers. But no amount of treatment could ever give him full recovery of his hands or stop the occasional tremor that flared through them. He'd never be able to work as a surgeon again.

For a while, he'd thought his medical career was over. But then a mentor had recommended that he give up his career in neurosurgery and re-specialize in obstetrics. As an obstetrician, the risk of his hand tremor affecting his patients was negligible.

It wasn't quite as glamourous as neurosurgery. It didn't provide the same excitement or thrill. But it offered other rewards. He'd been surprised to find how much he liked being able to form a connection between his patients and their families. Case in point, the small hands rummaging through the pockets of his white coat now, searching for chocolate.

"There's nothing in there, Manny," he said, meeting the guilty eyes of a ten-year-old who'd been caught red-handed. "But I've brought you something even better today. You have a baby sister."

Manuel Martinez wrinkled his nose. "A sister? What am I supposed to do with a sister? Girls are boring."

"You might not always feel that way," Bryce laughed.

The wrinkle stayed in Manny's nose. "Mother is going to name her Rosibel," he said. "It means kind, sweet and beautiful." The look he gave Bryce was full of disgust. "Can you believe it? The baby's already a girl, and now she's going to get a name that's even girlier."

"It's a pretty name, and very fitting," said Bryce. "Have you seen her yet? She's cute."

"I saw her," said Manny in tones of great despondence. Bryce guessed that it might be some time before Manny let go of his hope for a little brother. "She can't do very much."

"Well, she's only a few minutes old. Your expectations might be a little high. You know, you couldn't do very much, when you were born."

Manny gave Bryce a look indicating that despite his extreme skepticism, he would allow Bryce this illusion due to their deep friendship and mutual respect for one another. The boy had latched onto Bryce from the moment he'd arrived at the camp, and seemed to hero-worship him almost instantly. Bryce suspected that it was because Manny missed his father.

Manny gazed intently at Bryce and said, "Dr. Bryce, I thought that only women doctors delivered babies."

"That's simply not true," said Bryce. "Any kind of doctor with the right training can deliver a baby. It's a very important job."

Manny seemed to ponder this for a moment. "If we all start out as babies, then delivering them must be the most important job, because without doctors to deliver the babies, then there wouldn't be any more people."

"Sounds like a fair argument." Bryce would never admit aloud how much the boy's words bolstered him. It wasn't that he didn't think an obstetrician's work was every bit as important as a surgeon's. It was simply that every so often he had to fight back a small nagging feeling that he wasn't doing what he was meant to be doing. That obstetrics was a wonderful career, but ultimately, it was just a consolation prize. Most of his family and friends were surgeons, and although they had never said so outright, he couldn't escape the feeling that they all secretly pitied his inability to be the exemplary surgeon he'd once been. It was one more reason to get out of New York. In El Salvador, no one cared about who he used to be. No one expected him to be Bryce Hamlin, superstar surgeon. Medicine International had given him a chance for a fresh start.

"Will the new doctor who's coming be a woman?"

Bryce jumped up with a start and uttered something that made Manny bend over with laughter. "You have to put a coin in the camp swear jar, Dr. Bryce!"

In all his concern over Mrs. Martinez, he'd

completely forgotten that he'd been about to drive to the Miraflores bus stop to pick up the new doctor. Worse, it had never even occurred to him to tell anyone else that he hadn't left as planned.

And now the sun was dipping low on the horizon. Sunsets in El Salvador came fast. Fortunately, Bryce was pretty fast, too.

He ran across the camp to where Enrique was loading boxes of malaria vaccine onto a small white delivery truck.

"Enrique!" he yelled. "Did anyone pick up the new doc today?"

"I thought you did," Enrique said.

"I was about to, but then Mrs. Martinez went into labor, and I lost track of time."

Enrique stopped loading the vaccines. "Then you'd better take the milk truck. You'll never get back before dark, and you'll need some cover after nightfall."

"I can get there faster on my bike."

Enrique shook his head. "You and that bike. I know it's fast, but you seem to think it can perform miracles. Take the milk truck. We're supposed to get rain tonight."

But Bryce was already rummaging through one of the camp's outdoor storage trunks for a spare helmet. "The mountain villages need those vaccines," he said. "You said yesterday they're almost a week overdue."

"Then they can wait another day."

"Not an option," Bryce replied as they headed toward his motorcycle, parked just a few feet away. "No reason to do one task when we can do both. What's this new doctor's name?"

"I can't remember. I took a look at her file this morning, but our internet's been down all day and I can't log into the system. Are you *sure* you won't take the truck? It's slow, but it's reliable."

"My bike's reliable!" Bryce said, mildly offended. The motorcycle was his pride and joy, and he maintained it with loving care. It had never broken down, exactly, but he did have to be careful of hidden stones and tree roots whenever he tore along the unmarked jungle road that led from the camp to wider civilization. "She's already had to wait long enough. The least I can do is get there quickly."

Enrique looked at the sky, dubious. "And if it rains?"

"Don't worry. I'll get back here before you know it. Meanwhile, you can take the truck out to the mountain towns and come back in the morning." Bryce hopped astride the bike and snapped on a pair of heavy goggles in anticipation of the muddy road ahead. He started the engine and felt the thrill of anticipation that always came whenever he felt the motor thundering beneath him.

"You'll never make it back before nightfall," Enrique shouted above the noise of the engine. He was still shouting as Bryce gunned the engine of his motorcycle and took off at top speed.

Cassie trudged along the road, trying to find a positive side to her situation. The long walk gave her a chance to stretch her cramped legs after so many hours of travel. And the cool breeze against her face felt energizing. It would have been easier to focus on the positive if the straps of her backpack weren't digging into her shoulders quite so much, or if her feet weren't quite so sore.

Embrace the moment, she kept telling herself.

But it was hard to embrace the soreness in her feet. She tried to focus on the birdsong in the air, but was quickly distracted by another noise: an engine.

It sounded like a motorcycle engine. Even though it had been a long time since she'd ridden her own bike, she hadn't lost her ear for engines. This one sounded very well maintained. Whoever was riding it knew something about motorcycles.

The noise grew deafening as the driver burst from the rain forest on a very nice motorcycle, indeed. He was riding a Suzuki V-Strom 650, if she wasn't mistaken. One of the best bikes for rugged, unpredictable terrain.

As the rider pulled up beside her, his half-shaven face hidden by splattered mud and thick goggles, she allowed herself a moment to appreciate the aesthetics of such a beautiful machine. The body was powerfully built, gracefully compact and radiating an almost magnetic heat.

The bike was nice, too.

The rider simply sat next to her for a moment. Cassie felt as though he were staring, but she couldn't read his expression—the goggles completely covered his eyes. Was this the ride she'd been waiting for?

He cut the engine and eased his body off his motorcycle. He was six feet of lean, angular muscle. He wore a leather bomber jacket and jeans that hugged his thighs. And his clothes were streaked in mud. A shock of brown hair flopped over his forehead, which he pushed up as he casually lifted the goggles to the crown of his head, revealing deep-set brown eyes.

Eyes that Cassie recognized: pools of tenderness in an angular face.

Eyes she hadn't seen in five years. Not since medical school.

Eyes that belonged to...

"Bryce?" she said, not prepared for the well of emotion that sprang to her voice.

"Hey, Cass," he said. "Sorry I'm late."

CHAPTER TWO

CASSIE LOOKED THE SAME. The thought reverberated in Bryce's mind as he tried to absorb the shock. Five years had passed since he'd seen her, and yet she looked exactly the same. Her blond wavy hair was chopped into a short bob, and there were faint thin lines around her blue eyes. But they were unmistakably *Cassie's* blue eyes, and seeing them for the first time in five years sent the same jolt of electricity through him that he'd felt when they first met.

Recovering from the accident that damaged his hands had been hard, but recovering from Cassie had felt almost impossible.

And yet, somehow, he'd done it.

When he'd found her brief note on his nightstand, he couldn't believe she'd actually left. She was the first woman, the only woman, he'd ever been able to imagine a serious future with. He'd thought she wanted the same things he did: a life together, with the possibility of a family someday. Accepting that she hadn't wanted that was like trying to accept a knife wound to the heart.

At first he'd thought it was because of a decision they'd made that had led to disciplinary action for him at the hospital. She'd pushed him to perform a risky surgery, and even though he'd known he would face censure from the hospital, he ultimately agreed with Cassie that the risk was worth it. Unfortunately, the hospital board didn't see it that way, and he'd been denied his prestigious fellowship and placed on probation afterward. He'd known Cassie felt guilty about that, even though he had been the one to make the final decision. But the way she'd left—without even discussing it with him, just leaving a *note* and disappearing—made him realize that she wasn't simply feeling guilty about a risk they'd taken together. No, it had to be more than that.

Most likely, he'd been kidding himself about the depth of their relationship. Seeing what he wanted to see instead of what was actually there.

The more he'd thought about it, the more that had made sense. Cassie's boldness, the fearlessness with which she approached life, had been what attracted him to her at first. His own parents, both surgeons themselves, had been extremely overprotective. They'd seen countless trauma cases in the ER, and were always warning him of ways he could get hurt. Cassie, adventurous and unafraid of taking risks, had been a breath of fresh air. But the way she left had made him wonder if she'd ever really cared about him at all. Or if she was simply attracted to the excitement of their clandestine affair. Dating between medical students and residents was forbidden, after all. Their whole relationship had probably just been another thrill for her.

Her note had asked him not to call. And so he hadn't. Not even when, a few months later he'd been hit by that drunk driver. He'd spent years trying to put the accident and the breakup behind him. In El Salvador, he'd finally been able to piece together a life that wasn't overshadowed by anyone's expectations of who he used to be.

With Cassie standing in front of him now, a ghost from his past, he wanted to turn his motorcycle in the opposite direction and drive away. But he also found himself gripped by a perverse desire to gather her into his arms and feel the crush of her lips against his again.

Since neither of those choices were viable

options, he simply sat on his bike and stared at her.

He didn't think she could have raised her eyebrows any higher than they already were, but at his casual greeting, they somehow managed to gain another inch on her forehead.

"But how... What..."

He waited, trying to give her time to adjust to information that must surely be just as surprising to her as it was to him. He couldn't blame her for needing a moment to collect herself. At least he'd had a few extra seconds to prepare.

At last, she seemed to find her words. "Sorry you're *late*? Does that mean what I think it does?"

"If you're thinking that I'm here to pick you up, and that we're both going to be working together at the Medicine International outpost, then...yes."

She shook her head. "But that can't be. It just can't."

He would have loved to agree with her about the impossibility of the situation. But if there was one thing the past five years had taught him, it was how to accept situations that he couldn't change.

All he could do was move forward.

He tried to look as relaxed as possible, hoping Cassie wouldn't be able to see beyond his facade. Their situation was already difficult enough without her picking up on the conflicting emotions that were roiling in his chest. He didn't feel calm, but he tried to sound casual as he said, "I hope it's not the case that we *can't* work together. Otherwise, it looks like one of us is about to be out of a job."

For a moment, he thought she might be about to argue with him, and to his surprise, he almost wished she would. The blaze that flared up in her eyes stirred memories of all the things he'd liked the most about Cassie: her passion, her determination, her refusal to back down. But then, just as suddenly, her fiery expression changed into something he wasn't used to seeing on her face: caution, and even uncertainty.

Was Cassie Andover, the headstrong daredevil, actually hesitating? It wasn't the kind of reaction he'd ever expect from her. Typically, she'd act first and think later, trusting her gut and her instincts to guide her decisions. In the past, he'd envied her resoluteness. Of course, in the past, that resoluteness had left him heartbroken.

But she didn't need to know that.

He flipped the ignition switch on his bike, and the engine roared to life.

"The sun's going down," he said. "Are we going to stand here talking or are you going to get on this motorcycle so that I can take you back to camp?"

Cassie really wanted to get on his motorcycle.

Part of her was aching to do it. More than anything, she wanted to throw a leg over the bike and feel it thundering beneath her. Feel the wind against her face, the sensation of flying over the road.

But another part of her was remembering that the last time she'd rebelled against the rules of safety and caution she'd been taught as a child, Bryce was the one who had gotten hurt.

And now Bryce was in front of her.

She'd finally chosen to reconnect with her adventurous side, and right on cue, here he was. A reminder of everything that could go wrong when she threw caution to the winds.

Yet Bryce seemed different than he had five years ago. He certainly *looked* different. She wondered when he'd started working out. The white T-shirt underneath his open leather jacket didn't leave much to the imagination. He'd been fit when they'd dated, but now the outline of every muscle was visible through the shirt that stretched tightly across his chest. One of his triceps flexed as he rested his hand on the motorcycle's handgrip. Despite herself, she swallowed as the tan skin of his arms rippled with the movement.

The changes weren't merely physical. She couldn't put her finger on it, but his posture seemed more relaxed, more carefree. The old version of Bryce Hamlin had been sweet and funny. She'd often felt protective of him. This new version was someone she wanted to sink her teeth into.

She tried to steer herself away from such thoughts. It had been hard enough to find a way to live without Bryce for five years—*five years, three months and six days*, her brain helpfully reminded her—and she had no business thinking about Bryce's tanned skin now. Or his deep brown eyes. Or his hair. He'd always had great hair.

She shook her head. If they were going to be working together, she needed to keep her mind from going down this track.

For example, she really shouldn't be thinking about how it might feel to wrap her arms around Bryce's torso and press her body against his as they sped off into the forest together. That was exactly the kind of thought she didn't need to deal with right now.

But she did need to get on his motorcycle. There was no other way to get to the medical camp, and Bryce was already handing her a helmet that he'd produced from the storage compartment of his bike. She was so tired that she almost dropped it, and she couldn't help swaying where she stood.

"Hey." Bryce left the bike to idle on its kickstand and was at her side immediately. "Let's get this pack off you. That way you can sit down while I strap it to the bike."

The relief in her shoulders was glorious as he eased the giant backpack off her. It felt almost as good as the sensation of Bryce Hamlin's fingers brushing against her body for the first time in five years. Almost.

He took the helmet from her as well and tried to put it on her head. She leaned back from him, annoyed. "I can do it myself," she snapped, grabbing the helmet from him and adjusting the straps. Bryce's protectiveness reminded her of how people had once treated her as though she were made of glass. She didn't want that from Bryce, of all people. Especially right now.

Also, she'd had about as much physical

contact with Bryce as she could handle for the moment.

In her fatigued state, she thought that she was doing an admirable job of dealing with the shock of seeing Bryce, and the closeness of his physical presence, until he took off his leather jacket and handed it to her.

"Put this on," he said.

"Why?"

He gave her a fierce look. "Because you won't be safe riding without it. If you fall off, you'll need something to protect your skin. I've seen bikers come in to the ER with half the skin torn off their arms, and it isn't pretty."

This reminded her of the Bryce she knew. Cautious, planning ahead for every situation. Safety always came first with him.

As Cassie put on Bryce's jacket and the familiar masculine scent washed over her, she found herself inundated with memories. In a way, the good memories were just as painful as the bad ones. What might her life be like now, if she hadn't broken things off with Bryce? If she hadn't put his career and everything he cared about at risk?

It was a question that answered itself. Leaving him had been the only option. She could never ever have allowed Bryce to put his career at risk for her. There was nothing he loved more in the world than being a surgeon. She'd already cost him a prestigious fellowship, and she would never have been able to forgive herself if any further harm came to his career because of her.

But what was a surgeon as talented as Bryce doing working at an obstetrics clinic in El Salvador?

She wanted to ask him, but she wasn't sure if she was ready for the answer.

She eased herself onto the motorcycle behind Bryce and put her arms firmly around him. She'd come here to reconnect with her adventurous side, and she wasn't going to let the surprise of seeing Bryce again derail her from that plan. She was determined to find the excitement she'd come for.

"Ready to go?" he yelled over the engine, looking back at her.

She certainly didn't feel *ready*, but the sun was only getting lower in the sky.

"Let's do it," she said, and gripped him tightly as they sped into the jungle.

Bryce's thoughts felt as tangled as the roots and vines of the foliage that surrounded them as they sped through the trees. He was grateful that the unmarked road through the forest required his full attention. It spared his mind from being overrun by feelings he hadn't had to deal with for the past five years.

He felt Cassie's grip tighten around his waist, and he realized that he might be going just a little faster than he needed to. Still, he didn't slow down. The sooner they got back to camp, the better. Feeling Cassie holding tightly to his body brought back all the memories he'd come here to escape.

It had been a long time since he'd felt her arms around him. Anyone's arms, for that matter.

He needed to get the trip over with quickly. The sooner he didn't feel her body against his, the sooner they could shift into professional mode. They were two coworkers who happened to have a past, and nothing more. He needed to forget about everything they'd had together. After all, she probably had. It wouldn't be realistic or fair to expect that she'd spent the past five years ever thinking about him.

He gunned the bike faster, racing against the setting sun.

But as dusk fell, it became harder to see the road, as well as the treacherous roots and stones that lay in their path. Despite Bryce's desire to get their journey over with as quickly as possible, he knew he needed to slow down.

"What is it?" Cassie asked as he slowed to a crawl.

"I can barely see the road," he replied. "I don't want to—dammit."

The bike sputtered and choked.

"Come on, baby," he said to the bike. "Don't do this now."

But as he tried to press onward, the bike hit a loose stone, leading it to bounce and twist in the air. He heard Cassie shout and felt her body sliding behind him, and he braked hard and leaned back to prevent her from falling off the bike. She held on, but barely. Bryce cut the engine and parked the bike. He turned back to Cassie. "Are you all right?"

She'd pulled one leg up onto the bike's seat and was rubbing her ankle. "I'm fine, just jarred my ankle a little when we stopped."

"Let me see."

She jerked away from his touch with a fierceness that surprised him. "It's fine. It's just a little sore." She took off her helmet. "What's our situation?"

He frowned at the bike. "We hit that stone pretty hard. I think the engine's flooded." He tried to start the bike, to no avail. "I might need to take a look at the spark plugs." Cassie slipped off the bike and helped Bryce to remove her pack. He opened up the motorcycle's storage compartment, bringing out a small tool kit.

Cassie looked at the sun, low in the sky. "There's not much light to work by. How far is it from here to the medical outpost?"

"About five miles. The camp's fairly deep within the forest. It's close enough to town that we can get there easily to restock on supplies, but being in the forest gives us easier access to roads to the mountain villages. It's too far for us to walk tonight unfortunately. The trail's hard enough to see by day. We could get seriously lost in the forest. Not to mention the danger of running into animals or wandering into territory controlled by gangs. It's not worth the risk."

Although the light was dim, he could see by her expression that she had the same sinking feeling in her stomach that he did. "So if we can't get it fixed by nightfall…"

"We'll have to spend the night out here," he confirmed. "I've got a pop-up tent and a sleeping bag." *But only one of each*, he thought, but didn't say.

"What about those animals you mentioned? And gang members?"

"There's little chance of running into any

danger as long as we stay near the trail. Most animals will ignore us as long as we leave them alone. And we're close enough to the medical camp that I doubt we'll run into anyone who's not with our team… Although if we do, I should be able to talk us out of any trouble." He smiled, remembering Cassie's fondness for adventure. "Of course, I'm sure none of that would phase you."

Cassie took a few steps away, into the darkness. He guessed that she wanted a couple minutes to compose herself. He couldn't blame her. An hour ago, he'd never dreamed he'd be working with Cassie again, let alone facing the prospect of spending a night alone with her in the woods.

He turned back to the bike. "I think I can fix it. The only trouble is that it looks like it might—"

But before he could even finish his sentence, a fat raindrop plummeted from the sky onto his nose. Followed by several more. And then the sound of many more, hitting the tree leaves high overhead. Bryce estimated they had about two minutes to pitch the tent before they were both completely soaked. He was fast, but he wasn't that fast. He turned to Cassie, wondering how to break the news to her.

She said it for him. "We're going to have to spend the night out here, aren't we?"

"I'm afraid so. There's no way I can fix anything in this rain. I can barely see the engine."

She gave a curt nod and tucked the ends of her hair behind her ears as the rain began to plaster it to her head. *Funny*, he thought. At first, he'd felt a pang of regret that she'd cut her long hair, but as she tucked her locks behind her ears, he could see how the short bob suited the angles of her face.

"Bryce?" Cassie broke him out of his reverie. "If there's a tent, we'd better get it up now."

"Right." He retrieved the tent from the storage compartment, where it was bound into a compact square. It was large, but not that large. Two people would fit quite snugly, if they didn't mind sleeping close together. Very close.

Enrique was right, he thought. *I should have taken the milk truck.*

Cassie shivered inside the tent, cold and damp and fairly miserable.

Bryce had insisted that she take the sleeping bag. He was stretched out beside her, using his arm as a pillow. She, at least, had the luxury of burrowing down into the sleeping bag and bunching up the fabric beneath her head. It wasn't comfortable, but it was better than sleeping on the ground.

"You're shivering," he said. Damn. She'd hoped he wouldn't notice. But then, crammed inside the tent as they were, it was probably impossible to ignore even the slightest movement.

"I'm fine," she lied.

"You're not fine. Just being in the sleeping bag isn't enough. You need to get out of those wet clothes."

She would have loved nothing more than to get out of her wet clothes. In privacy. With some clean, dry pajamas to change into. And without her ex nestled firmly beside her in a small tent.

As long as you're wishing for things, you might as well add a million dollars and a pony to the list, she thought.

"What do you suggest?" she asked. "There's barely any room to move around in here. One of us can't go outside while the other changes." As if to prove her point, a clap of thunder broke overhead and the pattering of the rain on the canvas tent grew harder.

"Easy. I'll turn away, and you just sort of

shimmy out of whatever you need to from underneath that sleeping bag."

She frowned, skeptical. "I'm not sure there's enough room."

"I'll keep my back turned. Use the sleeping bag for cover. It'll be just like changing clothes at summer camp as a kid."

She wouldn't know. Summer camp, with all of its outdoor activities, had been deemed too risky for Cassie as a child. But she understood the gist of what Bryce was saying. There was just one problem.

"What about you?" she said. "You're soaking wet, and you don't even have a sleeping bag or a blanket."

"I can deal with it. I have before. Believe me, just having the tent is a luxury compared to some of the situations I've had to sleep in since coming here."

"I have a feeling that no matter what you've been through, *this* sleeping situation is one of the strangest."

A small smile crossed his face. "I have to admit that meeting you here, learning we'll be working together, and then sleeping together in close quarters on your very first night was not exactly how I thought the day would go."

She was glad to see that he felt the situation was as absurd as she did. But she couldn't let him shiver on the ground all night. She wouldn't be able to sleep, knowing that he was so uncomfortable.

There was only one thing she could do. "Bryce, I can't let you sleep on the ground in wet clothes while I'm dry in a sleeping bag. We're both adults. Just…strip down to your boxers, or whatever, and we can open up the sleeping bag like a blanket and share it."

He hesitated.

She mentally kicked herself. Less than an hour ago, she'd hopped onto the back of his motorcycle and promised herself that she'd still find her adventurous side, even with this new complication of seeing Bryce for the first time in years. But that wasn't meant to include convincing him to strip off his clothes and huddle next to her for warmth, without giving a second thought to how he might feel about it. She'd certainly spoken before thinking about how *she* might feel with him so close to her.

To her surprise, after a moment, he said, "Okay. I'll turn around, and we'll both do what we have to do. At least this way we'll have a chance of having dry clothes by morning."

Ten minutes later, Cassie found herself stripped down to her underwear, with Bryce in the sleeping bag behind her. The bag could fit them both, but just barely. They had to lie on their sides, and Bryce's arm was draped over her.

It felt surreal to be so close to him again. Still, Cassie had to admit that she was far more comfortable than she'd been a moment ago. It was a relief to be out of her wet clothes, and she was sure Bryce felt the same. As the warmth of their bodies heated the small space, it was almost pleasant to lie together, listening to the rain drumming on the canvas tent.

In such close proximity to Bryce, it was impossible not to notice that she was once again enveloped by the cedar spice scent of him. She took a deep inhalation as quietly as she could.

And then, in spite of herself, she started giggling.

She couldn't help it. Somewhere, far in the back of her mind, her physician self was running a mental self-diagnostic. *Sleep deprivation accompanied by fits of hysterics*, she thought. *Diagnosis—you've probably run into an ex while in the middle of nowhere.*

"Something funny, Cass?"

"It's just that earlier today I was talking to

a chicken, and now..." She couldn't finish, erupting into paroxysms of laughter again.

"I know," he said. He rubbed his hand briskly along her arm, comradely. "Weird day, right?"

"Yeah. Super weird." Her laughter fading. "Sorry. It's just that I haven't slept in twenty-four hours, and then when you showed up on that motorcycle...it was just so unexpected."

"I wasn't expecting to see you, either," he admitted. "I was just heading out to pick up the new doctor for the camp. I had no idea it'd be you."

His breath tickled her ear, and she felt another wave of worry. So much had happened, and they weren't even at the camp yet. There'd been no time for either of them to adjust to the shock of seeing each other again or to process the situation at all.

"Are we going to be okay working together?" she said.

"As I recall, we always worked well together."

"Until we didn't."

He groaned. "Cassie...it's in the past. We made the decision we made. And a lot has changed in five years. Can't we just focus on how to move forward?"

His breath tickled her ear, ever so slightly. He was so close she could almost feel his lips brush her skin. How long had it been since Bryce had held her this close?

Five years, three months and six days.

The whole point of breaking up with Bryce via note five years ago was that it had allowed her to flee his apartment without confronting him. Because she'd known that if she had to face him, he would convince her to stay. She wasn't proud of what she'd done. It had simply been what was required, in order for her to follow through with the breakup. The one thing she couldn't steel her resolve against was seeing Bryce in pain. And it was the thought that staying with him could result in even *more* pain that had spurred her onward all those years ago. She didn't know how he could look at her and not see the woman who had cost him a prestigious fellowship, and who had almost cost him his job. Who might *still* have cost him his job if anyone had found out they were dating. And so she'd left, knowing that she wouldn't be able to see him again without betraying both herself and him.

And now here he was, asking if they could move forward.

His body was so warm next to hers. His

arm settled so naturally around her waist. As though no time had passed since the last night she lay curled beside him.

Did she *want* to move forward? She supposed they didn't have a choice. Lying next to him and sneaking surreptitious inhalations of his scent was nice, but it didn't get them anywhere. They'd never be able to work together if she was still holding on to the past.

"You're right," she said. "We did work well together. And in spite of everything that's happened between us, the fact that you're here speaks well of the organization. They must be a very committed group of doctors to have you on the team."

"Very kindly said, Dr. Andover," he replied. "See? Just because we have a past doesn't mean we can't be professional."

"I agree," she said. "Although…maybe we don't need to tell our professional colleagues about tonight's sleeping arrangements."

"You read my mind."

After several minutes more, Cassie began to hear slow gentle snores from Bryce. She was glad he'd been able to get to sleep. She, however, was having more trouble.

Because it had been a long time since she'd

been nestled in someone's arms. And…it had been a while since she'd had sex…

Five years, three months and six days, in fact.

As she felt Bryce's body shift in his sleep, his arm tightened around her and pulled her closer to him.

Staying professional wasn't going to be easy.

No, it wasn't going to be easy at all.

CHAPTER THREE

THERE WAS A small commotion the next morning when Cassie and Bryce arrived back at the medical camp. Bryce's motorcycle had taken more damage than expected, and they'd had to walk the rest of the way with Bryce pushing the bike along. The ankle that Cassie had jarred when the bike had broken down still felt a bit tender, but she told Bryce she was simply footsore from walking so much the previous day. She knew if she mentioned her ankle to Bryce, he'd be concerned, and there was nothing she hated more than someone fussing over her. The last thing she wanted was for that person to be Bryce.

Dr. Enrique Garcia, the camp's director, met them at the entrance.

"I told you there'd be trouble with that motorcycle," he said, shaking his head at Bryce.

"It made more sense to take the bike than

the milk truck. The bike's faster," Bryce replied.

"Faster! Right, so much faster that you arrived twelve hours later than you planned. I can't imagine what kind of ramshackle operation our new doctor thinks we're running here." He turned to Cassie. "I can't tell you how glad we are to have you here, Dr. Andover."

Cassie shook his proffered hand. "Pleased to meet you."

"Cassie and I are actually...old friends," said Bryce.

If Enrique caught the hesitation in Bryce's voice, he didn't show it. "Let's get you settled in," he said. "I can assure you that despite the rustic appearance of our camp—" he waved an arm to indicate the cinder block walls and portable canvas medical tents in the forest clearing behind him "—we do have access to some decent amenities and technology. It's just that yesterday our internet happened to be down, and we were hit by a number of emergencies all at once, including a complicated breech delivery that Bryce got caught up in."

"Why would Bryce get caught up in a complicated delivery?" Cassie asked. "He's a surgeon, not an obstetrician." She turned around to look for Bryce, who was already striding across the camp.

"Need to check on Mrs. Martinez!" he called over his shoulder as he sauntered away.

He didn't have to leave so fast, Cassie thought. But then maybe he was just that eager to get away from her. Even after all their discussion of keeping things professional the night before, maybe Bryce still didn't know exactly how to get through the awkwardness of working together again. To be honest, she didn't know, either.

Enrique looked a bit taken aback. "Well, with Bryce otherwise occupied, I suppose I'll be the one to show you around."

"I could show her around." A boy of about ten had come to see what all the commotion was about.

"Not right now, Manny," said Enrique. "But why don't you run Dr. Andover's pack over to her living quarters for her? She's in block seven." Before Cassie could blink, the small boy flung her giant backpack over his shoulders and took off at full speed.

"Are there many children here?" asked Cassie as Enrique led her toward the nearest cluster of cinder block buildings.

"A handful. Manny seems to be their self-appointed leader for now. He's very curious, gets into everything—don't be afraid to be firm if he pesters you too much for chocolate, Dr. Andover."

"Duly noted. And please, call me Cassie."

As the tour continued, Cassie remembered that no one had answered her question earlier. "You said that Bryce was helping with a breech birth. Was there something so unusual about the case?"

Enrique looked at her quizzically. "No. Why do you ask?"

"Because you said that Bryce was called in," said Cassie, still wondering why they'd called a surgeon in to help.

"Yes, of course. Our midwives are incredibly skilled, but it's nice to be able to have an obstetrician on hand for complex cases."

"Bryce…is an obstetrician?"

"Of course. Almost all the doctors here are."

Her mind was spinning. She'd known the medical camp focused on providing services to new mothers and women giving birth, but somehow, when Bryce had picked her up on his motorcycle, she hadn't put the pieces together. She'd been so overwhelmed by seeing him again, by everything that had happened since she'd left home, that she hadn't bothered to think carefully about what Bryce's presence here might mean. He wasn't a surgeon anymore. He was an obstetrician.

Why wasn't he a surgeon anymore? Had he lost his job after she'd left him, after all? She couldn't think of anything on earth that would have led Bryce Hamlin to voluntarily give up surgery. Even Cassie, who had only been a medical student when they'd met, could see that Bryce was an artist in the operating room. And the passion had been evident on his face whenever he talked about his profession.

But even if he'd lost his job, why would he change specialties? Surely, he could have gotten a job as a surgeon somewhere else.

Was he no longer a surgeon because of her? Had she cost him everything, just as she'd feared she would?

She had to find out.

"Back when Bryce and I used to work together, he was a talented surgeon," she said. "Why would he change specialties?"

Enrique hesitated. "Bryce mentioned the two of you are old friends."

"Yes. We used to know each other well but…that was a long time ago. I haven't seen him in five years."

"Ah." The confusion lifted from Enrique's face, but he still seemed to be choosing his words carefully. "Then I suppose all I can say is that Bryce reached a point in his life where he needed a change."

That was probably true, but it was also frustratingly vague. Bryce had been a rising star in surgery. Why would anyone need a change from that? From Enrique's hesitant response, she had a feeling that if she wanted to find out, she was going to have to ask Bryce.

"I'm sure you and Bryce will have a great deal of catching up to do," Enrique continued, confirming her suspicions that she wouldn't get much information from him. "Personally, I'm just glad he's here. I don't think we've ever had a better obstetrician than in the three years he's been here."

Three years. No wonder it had been so easy to avoid news of Bryce. Early on, after the breakup, she'd tried not to hear any news of him through the medical community grapevine. But after a while, it seemed as though he'd disappeared completely. Now she knew why.

She pulled her focus back to the tour as Enrique pointed out the various buildings and features of the camp, though it was difficult to keep her thoughts from returning to Bryce.

"What kind of obstetrics cases come in?" she asked.

"We see a lot of Zika virus, but many of our patients are simply mothers who are undernourished, or who've been through enough harrowing experiences during their pregnancy that the fetus is at risk. It's hard to work without as much modern equipment as we'd like, but our medical team is great at improvising."

It sounded as different from Brooklyn General as she could possibly have asked for. Cassie felt a surge of excitement. *This* was medicine.

Enrique pointed out the shower unit somewhat apologetically. Six outdoor wooden shower stalls stood in the open air. A hose was rigged above each stall to approximate a showerhead. Cassie couldn't help feeling a twinge of longing for the luxurious steam-filled staff showers at Brooklyn General, with their organic jasmine soap and tea-tree-oil-infused shampoo.

"There's hot water," said Enrique encouragingly. "Although you'll want to shower early if you can, because it runs out pretty quickly. And you've really got to watch out for the door. It can swing open unexpectedly if the wood gets jostled even the tiniest little bit."

He showed her the dispensary, where staff

received any necessary medical care and daily doses of antimalarials. She made a mental note to return for a bandage and some pain relievers for her throbbing ankle as soon as the tour was over.

As they continued, she realized the camp was larger than she'd expected. It was fairly deep within the forest. Earlier that morning, as she and Bryce had been walking and pushing the motorcycle the last five miles to the camp, she'd barely been able to discern the road leading to the front gate. Enrique explained that the camp's relatively hidden location had a tactical advantage.

"We can travel wherever we need to in El Salvador, but it's best if the camp itself is in a location that's fairly out of the way, so that it won't become the target of a gang dispute," he said. "Plenty of the women and families here are escaping domestic violence situations or are seeking refuge because they're caught in the cross fire of territorial disputes. We're not exactly hiding, but we also don't want to be easily found."

"I've heard that gangs are a significant problem," Cassie said.

"One of the most challenging parts of our work involves dealing with the artificial borders created by gang activity," he said. "Different factions claim territory in the forest and in the mountains, and that makes it hard to deliver medicine and treatments to some of the people most in need. Of course, Bryce has been incredibly crucial in negotiating agreements so that our docs can travel where they need to, no matter who controls the territory."

Cassie wasn't certain she was hearing him correctly. Enrique made it sound as though Bryce negotiated with gang leaders on a regular basis.

"He has a surprising success rate," Enrique continued. "And for the mountain areas we absolutely can't get to, we can always do helicopter drops of medical supplies. Sometimes we'll have medical personnel drop down as well to perform a procedure. There are women who would have died if we hadn't been able to send anyone to help deliver the baby."

"You do helicopter drops here?" said Cassie.

"Oh, don't worry," said Enrique, mistaking her reaction for fear. "Bryce does most of those. We have a few other physicians who will do them, but most prefer keeping their feet firmly on the ground to jumping out of a helicopter. But you know Bryce. He loves that adrenaline rush."

"Right," said Cassie softly.

Gang negotiations? Helicopter jumps? Who the hell are we talking about? Because it's definitely not Bryce Hamlin.

Clearly, there was even more to the mystery of Bryce than she'd originally thought. Whatever he'd been doing over the past five years, it had involved a lot more than going to the gym. And she was determined to find out what it was.

The moment they'd arrived at camp, Bryce had welcomed the opportunity to head directly to the obstetrics tent, claiming the need to check on Mrs. Martinez. He needed space to think. Ever since he'd driven to the Miraflores bus stop yesterday and laid eyes on Cassie, he'd fought against the tension of two conflicting impulses.

He wanted to put as much distance as possible between himself and her.

He wanted to wrap his arms around her, hold her and never let go.

Sleeping next to her, practically naked in the cramped tent, hadn't exactly helped to resolve either of those impulses.

It had felt both sweet and frustrating to be so close to her. There were so many things he remembered that hadn't changed and yet felt completely new. The way his arm notched perfectly into the curve of her waist as he lay on his side, arm draped over her. The tiny divot in the nape of her neck.

But they'd both agreed to move forward, and thoughts like this would only serve to keep him stuck in the past.

Moving on hadn't come easily for Bryce, especially in the early days after the accident. When that drunk driver had swerved into his car, his life had changed forever. The physical recovery was hard, but giving up his career as a surgeon had been devastating.

His parents, grandparents and sister were all surgeons. They made jokes about surgery being the family business. Bryce hadn't always been certain he wanted to follow in their footsteps, but from the moment he first picked up a scalpel, he knew the operating room was where he belonged. Early on in his residency, he developed a reputation for being able to handle especially difficult cases that required singular patience and dexterity. Other doctors didn't merely praise his work, they described it with words such as *gifted* and *exceptional*.

Once, his father had sat in the operating theater and observed him working. "Son," he'd said afterward, "there are some people who are good surgeons. But you were *born* to be a surgeon."

At the time, his father's words had meant the world to him. But after the accident, the memory of that day was like a weight around his neck. If he was born to be a surgeon, and his hands had been permanently injured, then who was he supposed to be now?

His family and friends didn't seem to know how to support him. They made well-meaning comments about what a talented surgeon he'd been, but their words only served to remind him of everything he had lost.

Although no one said it outright, he could tell that some people from his past felt pity for him. Instead of being impressed by the new life he'd built for himself, they lamented the old life that he'd lost.

If Bryce were being truthful with himself, he missed that old life, too. He missed the life-and-death intensity of the operating room, the pride his family showed in him and the feeling of beginning an operation and knowing exactly what to do next. He missed being the person trusted with the most difficult, delicate cases. Surgery had provided all the excitement he needed in his life—or so he'd thought, until he met Cassie.

And now, she was in his life again. Here

to remind him of a version of himself that he hadn't been in five years. A version of himself that he was sick of competing with, and had done his best to escape.

He'd worked hard to build a new life in El Salvador. He took pride in being a good obstetrician, and he'd mostly managed to move beyond any longing he'd once had for his past.

Mostly.

Cassie's return had brought back so many memories of their time together, as well as the person that he used to be. But that's all they were: memories. He was tired of competing with his past self. The old Bryce needed to stay in the past, where he belonged.

Just as his relationship with Cassie needed to stay in the past, where *it* belonged. He felt again the tension of those two conflicting urges: to run from her and to hold her close. He couldn't run from her, so he'd simply have to ignore the desire to hold her the way he'd held her for warmth the night before. *That* certainly wouldn't be happening again. He would make sure of it.

Cassie had been brusque and businesslike when they'd woken in the morning to don their clothes. He still couldn't believe he'd agreed to strip down at Cassie's insistence. He had just been so cold after his dousing in the rain that he couldn't resist the prospect of getting warm. At least huddling together naked had given their clothes a chance to dry.

They'd have to be careful to avoid situations like that in the future. Especially if they were going to keep things professional, as they'd agreed.

But did he want to keep things professional?

He tried to tell himself the same thing he'd told Cassie last night: they needed to focus on moving forward. But it was hard to think about moving forward while he was being tantalized by the recent memory of her skin, dappled with raindrops, drying in the warmth of the sleeping bag.

It's just a physical attraction, he told himself. *She's always been a beautiful woman. There's no denying that.*

He could handle a physical attraction. He'd just give it a few weeks, and it would pass. Since the breakup with Cassie, Bryce hadn't been seriously interested in anyone. There had been a few casual encounters, but nothing that went far below the surface.

When he and Cassie had met, he'd been attracted to how daring she was. Growing up in a family of surgeons, Bryce had constantly been subjected to his parents' stories about patients who'd suffered serious injuries from accidents. From an early age, he'd learned to practice immense caution in order to prevent himself from becoming one of the victims in his family's stories. Then, when he'd finally become a surgeon, his family had repeatedly stressed the importance of avoiding any kind of injury to his hands. His hands were his living, his father had said. Any injury to them meant an end to his career. And his father had certainly been proven right about that.

Cassie's carefree nature had been a welcome contrast to his overprotective family. At first, he hadn't been certain of what to make of the headstrong woman who always seemed to be at the top of her medical cohort, eager to answer questions and ready to volunteer for any procedure. He'd noticed his attraction to her from the beginning, and he'd done his best to hide it. As a medical student, she was off-limits as a dating option, and he wasn't sure if she was even interested in him.

But then she'd invited him to meet her for coffee in the commissary. A simple cup of coffee seemed harmless enough. They'd talked about how they liked to spend the weekends. At the time, he'd preferred reading and listening to music. Safe indoor activities that kept his feet firmly on the ground.

Cassie, on the other hand, enjoyed rappelling. She headed to a state park every weekend to push herself off the cliffs.

Bryce had expressed his amazement at her willingness to drop off a cliff, only a rope between herself and certain death. "I could never do anything like that," he'd said.

"Sure you could," she'd replied. "I'll take you there some weekend on my motorcycle."

He'd sputtered a bit over his coffee. "Your *motorcycle*?"

Motorcycles were commonly referred to as *death traps* within the Hamlin family. His parents, both ER trauma surgeons, had shared many stories of motorcycle riders badly injured in accidents. He was pretty sure no Hamlin in three generations had ever ridden a motorcycle. And yet Cassie spoke of them as nothing more than an exciting mode of transportation.

"If there's one thing I could never see myself doing, it's riding a motorcycle," he'd said.

And yet, somehow, the next weekend found him tentatively getting onto a motorcycle behind her. To his surprise, the ride was freeing. With nothing surrounding him but the wind, and the road, and the closeness of Cassie, he felt much of his caution and worry drifting away.

He'd been exhilarated by the ride, but he was even more exhilarated afterward, when they'd gotten off the bike and she'd turned around and kissed him.

It had been a nervous, quick brush of a kiss, and he knew that she'd taken a risk by doing it. She hadn't been sure how he would respond. And he couldn't help himself. Despite the rules, he pulled her to him, and a kiss that had begun as tentative deepened into something much more.

After that, he spent much more time doing the kinds of things his family would have deemed too dangerous. There were many more trips on her motorcycle, as well as days spent riding roller coasters and rollerblading at skate parks. Things that he'd once found terrifying became thrilling when Cassie was there. There was an element of adventure she brought into his life that he hadn't known was missing.

She'd even talked him into doing karaoke. Never mind that he couldn't carry a tune. As it happened, neither could she. But he loved the way she belted out songs as though she meant them from the depth of her heart and soul—no matter how her audience might react.

Shortly after their last karaoke outing, he'd

bought the ring. He'd spent the night in tears of laughter, watching her give her hammiest performance of classic love songs in front of an obstreperous crowd. He'd been having so much fun, and then he'd realized that he never wanted to stop having fun with her. Or to be apart from her at all, really. And so he'd kept the ring close at hand, thinking that after she finished medical school, he might propose. But then the incident had happened.

Bryce and Cassie had been several hours into an ER shift. As senior resident, he was in charge; he was almost finished with the final year of his five-year residency as a surgeon. A patient had come in with an abdominal aortic aneurysm, a complicated procedure that only senior attending physicians at the hospital were allowed to perform. But by midnight, the attending physicians had all gone home. Bryce had put in a call for a senior surgeon, but with the terrible weather, several main roads were blocked and there was no telling when help would arrive.

"You have to do something," Cassie had said. "You know how to do the surgery. The aneurysm could burst any minute."

"It's against the rules," he'd replied. "What if something goes wrong? What if the patient dies because I took a risk?"

"He's guaranteed to die if you don't."

In the end, he'd compromised. Bryce informed the surgical nurses that instead of performing the full surgery, he would simply make an incision into the patient's abdomen large enough to expose the aorta. By starting the surgery, he could keep the patient alive until the attending physician reached the hospital. It was a bold plan, but it meant the patient was more likely to survive if the aneurysm ruptured while they waited for the attending physician.

The patient did survive, but the hospital board still felt it was necessary to take stern disciplinary measures. They attributed the patient's survival to luck rather than to Bryce's skill. As a medical student, Cassie had only received a warning, but as the resident in charge, Bryce had taken full responsibility for the decision and had been put on probation. If he made one more mistake, he would be fired immediately.

Bryce had told Cassie that it wasn't her fault. Ultimately, it was his decision, and even though they had broken the rules, they had also saved the patient's life.

He knew she felt guilty about pushing him to make the decision. But he had been the one to make the final call, and in spite of everything that had happened, he didn't regret it. The patient had survived and that was what mattered. If being put on probation was a consequence he had to live with, then he could handle that. He had a spotless record otherwise.

Cassie, however, was devastated that he was on probation. He was somewhat concerned, too, but he was reasonably sure that as long as they continued to keep their relationship a secret for a few more months, he wouldn't be fired. But to his great surprise, Cassie the daredevil, the fearless woman he thought he'd fallen in love with, was afraid to take the risk.

When she expressed her worries to him, he'd thought she simply wanted to lay low for a few months. Perhaps see each other less often until she graduated, just to play it safe for a while. But then he'd learned he lost a fellowship he'd applied for due to his probationary status. He couldn't hide his disappointment from Cassie.

Three days later, he found the note on his nightstand.

Sometimes he wondered if things between the two of them would have turned out differently if he hadn't been hit by a drunk driver six weeks later. His recovery had kept him from calling anyone at first. Only his immediate family had known what had happened, and he'd asked them to keep the news private. If Cassie knew about the accident, she might want to be there to support him. But he didn't want to have to deal with his feelings about her while he was also recovering from his injuries. And he definitely didn't want her pity.

And worse, what if she didn't come at all? Then he'd know for sure that the appeal of their relationship had never been that she was with him. Instead, it had been about the secrecy, the excitement and the danger of getting caught. A way to flaunt the rules, to get a thrill. That's what she'd been attracted to.

He'd held on to the ring for a while—longer than he thought he would—and then eventually sold it to pay for the Suzuki 650. A ring for a motorcycle. Not a bad trade, all things considered.

He'd been in El Salvador for three years, and in that time, he'd managed to build a life he could be proud of. He might not be a superstar surgeon, but he was a damned good obstetrician. And as for relationships…there had been a few flings, here and there, but no one serious since Cassie. He told himself that he preferred it that way. Life in El Salvador was complicated enough without romantic feelings getting in the way. Hell, practicing medicine was complicated enough without all that nonsense.

Which was why it was so important that he be able to accept that he and Cassie were two professionals with a past, and nothing more. Whatever physical attraction he might feel for her, it didn't change the fact that the two of them hadn't worked out, wouldn't work out and were never getting back together.

Realizing that he hadn't yet stopped by the dispensary for his daily antimalarial dose, he headed to the small cinder block building at the center of the camp. To his surprise, he found Cassie alone inside, struggling to wrap a bandage around her ankle.

"Are you okay?" he asked, alarmed. "What happened?"

She shrugged, dismissive. "It's no big deal. I just jarred my ankle a little when the bike jerked on that stone last night."

"Why didn't you let me look at your ankle? Why didn't you tell me something was wrong?"

She scowled at him. "Because nothing *was* wrong. It's not even a sprain. It's just a little tender and swollen. I'm only taping it up so it has a little support."

He looked at her ankle. It did indeed look a

little red and swollen, but not serious. Nothing that a little rest, support and pain relievers wouldn't cure. Cassie, however, had spent half the morning hiking back to camp. Why hadn't she said anything? Did she really feel the need to be so guarded that she couldn't even tell him when she was hurt?

Also, she was making a complete mess of the bandage. He'd had plenty of experience with sprained and stressed ankles, and he could think of at least three better ways to bind her foot that would offer more support.

"I would have appreciated you letting me know that you'd been hurt," he said. "Especially with all the walking we did this morning. I could have helped you."

She rubbed her ankle and undid the bandage again. "I don't need help."

He looked at where the bandage lay unspooled around her foot. Despite his frustration at her for not telling him about her injury, he couldn't help smiling at her clear difficulty with the bandage.

"Is that so? Because I've seen first-year medical students provide better first aid than this. Are you sure you're a doctor?"

Her eyes sparked. "I'm an ob-gyn, not a physical therapist. I haven't needed to tape up an ankle in years."

He sat beside her. "Come on, let me take a look. I've had to take care of plenty of my own bumps and bruises since I got here. You develop a knack for it after a while."

Grudgingly, she handed him the bandage. He probed her ankle, looking for tender spots. After he'd ascertained for himself that Cassie's injury wasn't serious, he wrapped the bandage around her ankle and her foot, creating a makeshift splint.

She flexed her foot, testing. "That actually feels a lot better. Thank you." Then she looked rather shamefaced. "Look… I'm sorry if I was giving you a hard time. The truth is, I absolutely hate being fussed over."

He knew the feeling. It was often hard, as a doctor, to be in the patient role. Bryce always felt slightly uncomfortable whenever he needed any sort of medical attention of his own. He smiled at her. "Fiercely independent, as ever." And then, although he tried to stop himself, he couldn't help adding, "Is it worth it?"

"Is what worth it?"

"Proving that you don't need any help. From anyone." *Especially not from me*, he didn't say, although the words hung unspoken in the air.

She thought for a moment, and he cursed

himself for letting his words slip out. Why couldn't he have simply accepted her thanks, instead of making the moment so awkward? What could he possibly expect her to say?

She took a deep breath. "There's something about me that I've never told you."

Something in her tone made him pause. Whatever it was she was working up to, it seemed as though it were difficult to get out. He regretted his sharp words from a moment ago. Cassie was the one with the hurt ankle, and he'd just made the situation worse.

And yet he did want to know why she was so determined to prove that she didn't need anyone's help. It certainly wasn't getting her anywhere—look at what a mess she'd made of that bandage.

He recalled his physical therapy after the accident. There had been so many times when he'd wanted to be independent. He'd hated having to admit that he was at his limit, and that he needed to ask for help from someone else.

But he'd learned to do it. What was keeping her from doing the same?

Her next words took him by complete surprise.

"I was born with a heart defect. I had three surgeries before I was sixteen."

It was not the turn he'd expected the conversation to take. Not by a long shot. "Why didn't you ever tell me?"

"I hardly tell anyone. It's the kind of thing that can make people think differently about me once they know it. And I didn't want that to happen with you. It might sound silly, but… I didn't want you to see me as weak."

"Weak? Why on earth would I think that?"

"Sometimes people react that way. Even though I'm healthy now, sometimes people start treating me as though I'm excessively fragile when they find out." Her eyes met his, and he saw their familiar blue blaze burning. "I never wanted *you* to see me that way. As someone who needed extra protection or as this dainty, fragile object, always a moment away from breaking. I never wanted you to see me as anything less than capable."

"No one who knows you could ever think that." He held her gaze for a moment longer than he meant to. Could she really think that he would ever see her as weak? Nothing could be further from the truth.

He'd seen the same fire in her eyes in the past. It blazed whenever she was arguing a point or advocating for a patient…or whenever she was at her most passionate. He looked away and cleared his throat. "So that's why you need to show you can do everything on your own. You need to prove that you're more than your diagnosis."

"I've always wanted to be. But ever since I was born, my diagnosis ruled my life. When I was in school, my nickname was Heart Defect Girl. My entire identity was reduced to my heart condition."

He winced. "Children aren't always good at making sure everyone feels included."

"You'd be surprised at how adults aren't all that different."

He nodded slowly. Cassie's news was unexpected, but it also made certain things click into place. He remembered how she'd snapped at him yesterday in the forest when he'd offered to look at her ankle. He'd only meant it as a thoughtful gesture, but Cassie had probably chafed against what she'd perceived as overprotectiveness.

Other things were clicking into place, as well. He remembered how she had always jumped into things with both feet, whether it was a complicated birthing procedure or the longest, loudest song at a karaoke bar. Had all the risks she'd taken during their relationship been her way of proving that she wasn't fragile?

He thought about how his own childhood had been full of activity. He'd leaped off swings, jumped on trampolines, played sports. All things that children with healthy hearts could do without a second thought. He couldn't imagine what it would feel like to have to constantly sit on the sidelines, watching everyone else have a normal, active childhood.

"It must have been hard to miss out on so much."

She sighed. "Missing out was bad enough, but my parents treated me as though I were made of glass. Everyone was constantly telling me what *not* to do so that I wouldn't put a strain on my heart. Even things that were normal for other kids were deemed too dangerous for me. You mentioned summer camp last night. I've never been to summer camp in my life. I couldn't climb trees. I couldn't ride bikes. Hell, after I had my last surgery, there were a few weeks where I was so weak I couldn't even tie my own shoes."

"I bet all of the rules and restrictions were suffocating."

"Actually, all of that overprotectiveness backfired. I promised myself that as soon as I was strong enough, I'd never let anyone tell me anything was too dangerous ever again." She smiled ruefully. "And then I went to medical school and got my big chance. My heart was finally completely healthy. I was living on my own for the first time in my life."

"And you wanted to seize the day." All of this explained a lot. But it also made him consider Cassie in a new light. He'd always thought her fearlessness was an inherent part of her personality. But the information about her heart defect put everything in a different context. Now he found himself wondering if she wasn't such a natural risk-taker, after all. Instead, she'd been pushing herself to take risks. Somehow, thinking about her in this way gave him an unexpected pang of warmth for her. For the small girl Cassie had been and the young woman who had been trying so hard to prove herself.

Her next words confirmed his hunch.

"Carpe diem, indeed. Half the reason I argued so much with the other residents and attending physicians was because the feeling of going against authority was so new to me. From the outside, I looked like a med student advocating for her patients, but inside I was basically a teenager who saw rules as something to be broken."

He couldn't stop himself from asking. "Was our relationship another opportunity to break the rules?"

She looked as though he'd slapped her. "Wait a minute. Is that what you think? That our relationship was just about me getting a thrill?"

He shrugged. "I get it. You'd been sheltered your whole life and were chafing against the rules, understandably so. And you decided to use me as one more way to rebel."

For a moment, her eyes blazed, but then she grew thoughtful. "That was part of the appeal at first," she admitted. "But only at the very beginning."

What did she mean by *only at the very beginning*? Did she mean that she'd eventually developed deeper feelings for him later on? Or that the appeal had faded and she'd ultimately viewed their relationship as a mistake? He wasn't sure he wanted to know.

She was staring at him as though she expected him to say something. But his mind was spinning with questions, and his heart was full of a feeling he couldn't name. All he could manage to say was, "Everybody has regrets."

"Well, I regret the way I left. I shouldn't have left a note. I should have talked things over with you, ended it face-to-face. For all the risks I took that year, I should have at least been able to handle that. But I couldn't and… I'm sorry."

She was trying to move on, he realized. She was trying to do exactly what they'd talked about last night: find a way to move forward, as professionals. Maybe even as friends.

He realized she was still watching him for some response. He decided that if she could move forward, then he could, too.

"Apology accepted," he said, and he found that the words did leave him feeling as though a weight had been lifted from his chest.

But any relief he felt was short-lived. Because the moment the tension in his chest eased, he found himself confronting a new problem.

He no longer struggled with the two conflicting impulses that had been tearing him apart since she first arrived. That problem was solved. Because the urge to run from her was gone.

But the impulse to gather her into his arms was stronger than ever.

Apparently, moving on was going to be harder than he'd thought.

CHAPTER FOUR

CASSIE SPENT THE next few weeks adjusting to life at the camp. Because her patients came from such varied situations, each day was different, and she never really knew what was in store for her when she began her work in the morning.

The camp was unlike any setting she had ever worked in. It was difficult not to have modern medical equipment, but she also found that the limitations she faced made her rise to the occasion and work harder than ever before. During each delivery, she had to keep her attention focused in numerous directions. Without a monitor to alert her of when a fetal heart rate was dropping or a pulse oximeter to measure oxygen levels in a patient's blood, she had to rely on her training and her observational skills, and she couldn't afford to lose focus for a second.

Delivering babies had always held its share

of drama. If something went wrong, it meant tragedy for everyone involved. The despair of losing a new life or of a mother being at risk, all of it was the price Cassie paid for the other side of obstetrics: the side filled with celebration and joy. But practicing in El Salvador raised the stakes to a whole new level. The more Cassie saw of the struggles that her patients faced, the more she felt that she was in the right place. Her patients wanted what any parent wanted: to give birth in a safe place, with the best care available. Cassie was determined to offer them that in any way she could.

She found herself rediscovering some of her most deeply held beliefs as a physician. She'd started her career in medicine with the dream of showing each patient the same kind of personalized care her family had received when she was a child. Each doctor who'd operated on her heart had taken the time to get to know her family and had closely followed Cassie's recovery afterward. But by the time she'd graduated medical school, the landscape had changed. Many of the hospitals with the most resources were private hospitals, where the administration's focus was on the bottom line. That meant less time spent with patients and more pressure to complete as many billable procedures as she could each month. She'd chosen to work at a private hospital so that she could provide her patients with the best care possible, but she wasn't sure, now, if it really was the best care. There was so much focus on profits that she'd felt more like a baby delivery service than a real doctor.

And for a long time, she'd accepted that as the way of things. She hadn't started out that way. Back when she'd been a medical student who pushed herself to be fearless, she was a fierce advocate for her patients. If she felt that one of her patients needed extra time or care or a risky procedure, she wouldn't hesitate to fight on her patient's behalf. But she'd buried that part of herself behind after she'd left Bryce, blaming her outspoken, adventurous side for causing so much trouble.

Working at the camp was making her wonder how she could have gone for so long without challenging the status quo. That young rebellious version of herself hadn't been afraid to go against the system or take unorthodox steps if she felt she needed to advocate for the well-being of her patients. At some point, she'd lost sight of that person, but as she spent more time working at the camp, she realized that this was a setting in which risk and improvisation were far from discouraged. In fact, they were viewed as a necessary part of providing care. She was reconnecting with her passion for medicine, just as she'd hoped she would.

She also found that she was reconnecting with Bryce. It was impossible for them to avoid running into one another in such a small camp, and they often worked on the same cases together.

It was so easy to fall back into a steady rhythm of working with him. She'd forgotten how well they'd collaborated, but as they shared more cases, they resumed their natural tempo as though the years hadn't passed. They worked together seamlessly, especially during difficult or complex cases that required taking medically necessary risks, as well as exercising extreme caution with the same patient. The patients who needed more risky procedures were often the most fragile, and Cassie noticed that she and Bryce balanced each other out especially well with these cases.

She still hadn't found out why he'd become an obstetrician. Somehow, she couldn't get up the nerve to ask him outright. There was so much she didn't know about what had happened to Bryce over the past five years. Had he ultimately lost his job after she left? Even if he had, why would he give up surgery?

And the conversation she'd had with Bryce as he'd bandaged her ankle continued to reverberate in her mind. His words had cut her to the bone.

Was our relationship another opportunity to break the rules?

At first, she couldn't believe he'd think that of her. He made it sound as though to her the relationship had just been some meaningless fling, a chance for her to rebel. But as their conversation continued, she'd realized, horrified, that he did see it that way. And worse, she could understand why.

She'd left her short, terse little note because by giving up Bryce, she felt as though she were giving up everything. She couldn't find the words she needed to say to him, and she knew she wouldn't be able to go through with it if she saw the pain on his face. But when he'd lost his fellowship…she couldn't stand to hurt his career anymore. Leaving him was the hardest decision she'd ever made.

But she realized now that Bryce hadn't understood that at all. He thought she'd left because she didn't care about him. He thought, now that she'd had the fun of a secret relationship, she'd dashed off the note and left because the relationship had never been that important to her in the first place.

And now she didn't know if there was any way she could convince him to see things differently. To make him know just how much she cared.

In order to go through with the breakup, she'd tried to convince herself that giving up Bryce was the right thing. The brave thing. But after hearing Bryce accuse her of taking their relationship lightly, after learning that he believed she'd just been enjoying a fling, she had to admit that the way she'd handled the breakup hadn't been brave at all. Instead, she'd just been afraid.

As far as she could tell from Enrique and their other colleagues, fear was not an emotion that Bryce struggled with. Apparently, he volunteered for daring missions into the mountain territory as often as possible. That was something unexpected about him, as well. The Bryce she remembered had been exceptionally cautious, careful and measured. Why had he changed?

Manny Martinez, the child who'd carried her backpack to her room on the day she arrived, held a wealth of information about Bryce. The boy seemed to hero-worship Bryce and followed him everywhere, although he

often tagged along with Cassie and ran errands for her when she made her morning
rounds. He enjoyed regaling her with stories
of Bryce's exploits, many of which had clearly
been enhanced by Manny's imagination. For
example, she didn't believe that while traveling miles to deliver medicine to a remote village, Bryce and Manny had crossed a river
by stepping on the backs of crocodiles, only
to be accosted by a nest of snakes when they
reached the other side. She expressed her
doubts to Manny, with the result that he dou-
bled down and implied that jaguars may have
been involved, as well.

He'd proudly shown her Rosibel, his newborn sister, at the first opportunity. Apparently, Bryce had delivered the baby on the
day Cassie arrived in El Salvador.

"I wanted a brother, but girls aren't all
bad," Manny said. "Mama is so busy taking
care of Rosibel that she never even notices
how many pieces of chocolate I have." The
grin on his face suggested he was making the
most of his mother's distraction, and Cassie
noticed that his pockets bulged with sweets
pilfered or begged from other doctors.

Cassie held her finger out to little Rosibel now as she checked in on the mother and
baby. The baby instantly closed her tiny hand

in a firm grip. So Bryce had brought this sweet baby into the world. Bryce the obstetrician, not Bryce the surgeon. There was something about a newborn that always made her feel hopeful. A new life with so much possibility ahead. When Cassie had been born, everyone had been afraid for her. But in spite of everything, she'd focused on pursuing life as vigorously as she could. For her, that was what delivering babies was all about: focusing on life. And now Bryce was delivering babies, too.

Who was this mysterious man who apparently delivered babies one day and jumped onto the backs of crocodiles the next?

There was so much she didn't know about him.

Over the past five years, whenever she'd thought about Bryce, she always pictured the man she'd known in the past. She'd never thought that he might change.

But of course he had, and she knew that she shouldn't be surprised. They were both different people than they used to be.

She'd always been drawn to his tenderness. She recognized it in the solicitous way he'd helped her bandage her ankle and the patience he exercised with Manny. But now there was also a toughness to him that she'd never expected. She noticed it whenever she saw him tearing away from the camp on his motorcycle or shouting orders to medical teams as they prepared for a new influx of refugees. The same tenderness she'd always seen in him was still there, but now it was balanced with a rugged determination to do whatever it took to get a job done.

She found it damned attractive, if she were honest with herself.

She'd seen glimpses of that determination when she'd watched him work as a surgeon.

She wondered again why he'd ever given up surgery. It was such a vastly different process from obstetrics. In surgery, patients were usually anesthetized, and the skill lay entirely in the doctor's hands. But delivering babies was a team effort. The patient's role was every bit as active as the doctor's, often more so. Building trust between the patient and medical personnel was crucial, especially if the patient was scared or if things weren't going as expected.

Why would Bryce, a masterful surgeon, seek out such a different experience? What had made him change?

It could have been anything. Five years was a long time. Perhaps he'd met someone else who'd inspired him to switch to obstetrics?

Another thought settled into her stomach like a block of ice. What if switching specialties hadn't been Bryce's choice at all?

Changing specialties was no small feat. He would have had to redo his residency, probably at a completely different hospital.

She could think of only one reason why Bryce might have needed to move to a different hospital and redo his residency. Thanks to her, he'd been on probation when she'd left the hospital. Another mistake could have cost him his job.

For example, if anyone had found out that he'd dated a medical student, it might have been the final straw for Bryce. That was why she'd left—to avoid causing him any more pain.

But what if someone had found out? What if, despite everything she'd given up by leaving him, Bryce had been fired because of her, after all?

But if he had been fired, wouldn't he have been able to finish his residency somewhere else? He'd been such a talented surgeon. Any hospital would have been lucky to have him. Surely, she couldn't have ruined his career that much… Could she?

She needed to know. Even if she didn't like the answer, she absolutely needed to know if

Bryce had lost his job and put himself through the ordeal of changing specialties because of her. Because despite what Bryce might think, their relationship had been important to her. She'd left him in order to protect him, hoping not to cause any more damage to his career than she already had. And even if there was nothing she could do about it now, she needed to know if she'd ruined his career. And if she had, she'd find a way to make it up to him. Somehow.

Bryce was surprised when Cassie showed up at the front door of his quarters, asking if he wanted to join her in the mess hall for a morning coffee. He was even more surprised when he found himself saying yes.

Slipping back into professional mode with Cassie had turned out to be far easier than he'd thought. He found he enjoyed working with her as much as ever. In fact, all the things he'd missed about working with her had come rushing back. The banter over patients and the ease with which they anticipated one another's decisions was refreshing after the years they'd spent apart. And he had to admit that despite himself, his curiosity had continued to burn after their conversation in the dispensary. He'd never known that

Cassie had a heart defect. She had kept that information from him all that time.

Before the accident, he might not have understood her choice to keep the secret. But he could understand all too clearly now. For so long, his family had seen him only as the superstar surgeon. They'd focused on that one single part of him so much that when his life changed, they could only see what he'd lost. Sometimes it was still hard for Bryce himself to see that he was more than his past.

Cassie wanted to keep her heart condition private for the same reasons he wanted to keep the accident and his former career as a surgeon private. Once people knew something so serious, there was a chance they might only view you through that lens. He didn't want to be known as a person who used to be a gifted surgeon. That wasn't his identity anymore. He'd fought hard to become more than an accident victim, more than someone who *used* to be something.

It sounded as though Cassie had also been fighting to be seen as a whole person and not just one thing.

He remembered what she said her childhood nickname had been—*Heart Defect Girl*. What must it have been like for her to constantly feel singled out like that?

He wondered what else she hadn't told him.

When they reached the mess hall, he got their cups of coffee while she waited. When she put her cup to her lips, she smiled. "You remembered just how I like it."

"Black, with two sugars. There are some things about Cassie Andover that you don't forget. How she takes her coffee is one of them. Not if you know what's good for you."

"We've got a lot of memories, don't we, Bryce?"

He returned her smile. "We do. And I'll even go as far as to say that most of them are good ones."

She was silent for a moment, then cocked an eyebrow over her cup of coffee. "Agreed. But I didn't ask you here this morning to talk over old memories. I want to solve a mystery."

He waited, wondering what she was getting at. "As you may remember, I do love a good mystery."

She set her cup down. "That's the thing, Bryce. I *do* remember that about you. And you remember how I like my coffee. So clearly you are the same Bryce I dated five years ago."

"Who else would I be?"

"That's the mystery we're here to solve. The Bryce I remember had to be begged to get on my motorcycle back in New York. He didn't have one of his own, and if he did, he'd *never* have driven it the way you drove yours when you picked me up a few weeks ago. The Bryce I knew loved being a surgeon and couldn't imagine any other career. He didn't jump out of helicopters or negotiate with gang leaders. And he sure as hell never wrestled any crocodiles in any sort of man versus reptile death match."

"Ah, I see you've been talking with Manny." Bryce wondered if Cassie had been seeking out information about him from the boy or perhaps even from some of their other colleagues. Did that mean he'd been on her mind? Just like she'd been on his.

"Manny's cute. Don't change the subject. Who are you and what have you done with the Bryce I used to know?"

Bryce slowly stirred his coffee, wondering how to answer. Of course, his life had changed since the accident and since giving up his career as a surgeon. But he hadn't thought that he had changed that much as a person, until now. He supposed Cassie had a point. He *had* been reluctant to do anything risky back when they'd dated. One of his favorite things about her had been her ability to pull out his adventurous side from wherever it was hidden.

It had also been one of the reasons he was so devastated when she left.

As he wasn't quite sure how to answer her, he stalled for time instead. "It's been five years, Cass. That's a pretty big question."

"Then start at the beginning. No, actually, start with what I really want to know. How the *hell* could you afford such a beautiful bike on a Medicine International salary?"

Typical Cassie. Cutting straight to the heart of things without even realizing it. He'd been enjoying their renewed connection over the past few weeks, but he wasn't sure he was ready for this conversation. In fact, it might be because of their renewed connection that he didn't want to simply blurt out the full story of how he'd come by his motorcycle— that he'd bought it by selling the ring he'd meant to propose to her with.

The trouble was, he'd never been a very good liar. And since their breakup, he'd gotten even worse at it. His hand tremor flared any time he lost control of his emotions. Cassie wouldn't know to look for it, but if his hands wavered, if she noticed and asked him about it…he had no idea how he'd respond.

He decided to offer up half the truth.

"I was dating someone a while back and saved up for an engagement ring. But it didn't work out. Sold the ring, bought the bike. Not much else to tell." He shrugged, trying to keep his body posture casual. It was all true. He was simply neglecting to mention that the ring had been meant for Cassie. A small extraneous detail.

She choked on her coffee. "You almost got engaged? Then you weren't just dating—it must have been serious."

"I thought so, but I guess she didn't."

"What was her name? What was she like?"

Bryce paused. He hadn't intended to tell Cassie any outright lies. He'd been hoping he could get away with simply omitting certain truths. He was relieved when she continued, "Actually, scratch that. You don't have to tell me anything you don't feel like talking about. Whatever happened, I'm probably the last person you'd want to rehash all of it with. I only invited you to meet here because I wanted the two of us to have a chance to talk about *us*, about our..." She seemed to be struggling to find the right words.

"Our friendship?"

"Yeah," she said. "Our friendship. It's such a small camp, and we see each other every day. And aside from the initial shock of seeing you on my first day, now that I've had some time to adjust… I really like it here. The only thing that could possibly make life better would be if the two of us could be friends. But in order to do that, we'd have to get to know each other again, don't you think?"

She was right. They'd both changed. He probably was a bit more reckless than he used to be, especially as he didn't have to obsess over protecting his hands anymore. And he'd always thought of her as bold, adventurous. But now he'd learned that those qualities didn't come naturally for her. She'd had to work to find them. He wondered if she'd been able to keep in touch with her adventurous side over the years since they'd been apart.

She was right. They needed a chance to get to know each other.

"You're not the only one with questions, you know," he said.

"I'll answer yours if you answer mine."

"Okay. I'll go first. What's the best ob-gyn in New York City doing in El Salvador?"

Her burst of laughter surprised him. "Did I say something funny?"

Her eyes sparkled. "I think I laughed because your question answered itself. My job in New York is what drove me straight here. And I don't know that I was the *best* ob-gyn."

"Come on, don't be modest. My friend Marcus's wife said she couldn't even get an appointment with you. The scuttlebutt is that you have to know someone who knows someone if you want to get an appointment with Cassie Andover."

She rolled her eyes. "Ugh, that's exactly why I came here. I never meant for it to be that way."

"But there has to be some truth to it, otherwise you wouldn't have earned that reputation."

"Maybe. But honestly, sometimes I think my entire reputation is a fluke. I was just in the right place at a significant time in someone's life."

"How so?"

"A few years ago, there was a car crash off the interstate. One of the survivors was a pregnant mother who started going into premature labor. She also happened to be a very famous singer. I delivered the baby, word got around and suddenly I was working more and delivering some very wealthy babies into the world. Which meant dealing with some of the most demanding parents I've ever met. And the more money they have, the more demands they have. They treated me and my nursing staff like servants."

"Sounds like you needed a change."

"Exactly. And so—" she spread her arms out to indicate the mess hall and the rest of the medical camp "—here we are."

Suddenly, her eyes flickered in recognition. "Did you say *Marcus's* wife wanted to get in to see me? Marcus, from the old hospital? God, I haven't seen Marcus since—" her face broke into a grin "—since the last day of his surgical rotation, when you dared him to drink from that phlebotomy sample cup."

"I did not *dare* him... I kindly *offered* him fifty dollars to drink whatever I might have happened to put in the cup."

"Which happened to be a pale yellow liquid."

"As I recall, you were the one who walked away with the fifty dollars."

Cassie scoffed. "It was obviously apple juice."

"But you had no way of being sure."

She smirked at him. "I trusted you. For the most part. I'm surprised Marcus didn't. He could have made a quick fifty bucks."

"The face he made when he saw you drinking what he thought was a urine sample was pretty priceless. Well worth fifty dollars."

"Poor Marcus. We were pretty relentless with the pranks."

"We all were," he said. "Marcus got back at me by putting surgical lube on my stethoscope ear tips. That was just delightful to put into my ears, let me tell you. And I remember a time when it wasn't safe to fall asleep in the staff room because you'd wake up finding that someone had put a plaster cast on one of your arms or legs."

They'd had a lot of fun, roping one another into hijinks back when they'd worked together. Bryce had always felt passionate about medicine, but it was also something he'd approached very seriously. Cassie had added something to his passion. She'd made working at the hospital fun.

"I miss things being so easygoing," she said. "Brooklyn General's a lot more uptight than our old hospital. There's no tolerance for pranks. With our clientele, all of the focus is on meeting their demands. No one has the time or energy to let loose."

"So you haven't pulled any death-defying stunts lately? I thought for sure I'd hear about you delivering a baby while white-water rafting by now."

"Only if it becomes the next celebrity birthing craze. Which wouldn't entirely surprise me. In fact, keep that thought to yourself—don't give my patients any ideas."

"That bad, huh?"

She shook her head. "I was working so much that I could barely tell my days apart anymore. I wanted something that would let me slow down and get in touch with what really mattered. Whatever that might be."

Now it was his turn to raise an eyebrow. "Only you would come to a country with twenty active volcanoes to slow down."

"Hey, that's not fair! I've actually become fairly responsible over the years."

He snorted. "I'll believe that when I see it."

"But you've changed, too. Tell me about this new Bryce who jumps out of helicopters."

"It doesn't happen that often. Maybe four times over the past year."

"Even *once* a year is just very…different from the Bryce I used to know. But it's not just the idea of you jumping into danger that surprises me. You changed specialties. Why on earth would you do that? That's huge, that's not something one does on a whim. Especially as you were such a talented surgeon."

He cringed inwardly. There they were, the words he dreaded most: you *were* talented. The words he'd come to El Salvador to avoid ever hearing again.

He reminded himself that Cassie didn't

know about the accident. She couldn't know how much of the past was a sore spot for him.

For a moment, he thought about coming out with the whole story. The crash, the tremor it had left in his hands and how he didn't have to worry about preventing injuries anymore because protecting his hands didn't matter as much as it used to. But something stopped him. Cassie had clearly heard some stories about some of the more dangerous things he'd done since coming to El Salvador. There was a familiar light in her eyes, an eagerness she remembered from the old days. He'd seen a flicker of it when he'd picked her up and insisted she get on his bike.

He couldn't quite bring himself to tell her that he hadn't turned into some sort of adventurous medical version of Indiana Jones. He didn't take on the camp's more dangerous duties because he craved excitement. He did it because it simply didn't matter if he got injured anymore. He wasn't brave; he just didn't care if he got hurt.

But even though years had passed, even though the way she felt about him shouldn't matter anymore…for some reason, he didn't want her to stop looking at him the way she was right now. As though he were someone who was fearless.

He told himself he was being ridiculous. The way Cassie looked at him shouldn't matter. It *hadn't* mattered for years, and he'd gotten along just fine without giving a moment's notice to what she might think of him. So there was no reason for him to hesitate in giving her the truth now.

He opened his mouth, about to explain, when the doors of the mess hall burst open and Anna, the midwife, rushed in. "We've got a complicated delivery in tent three," she said. Bryce noticed she was somewhat breathless. She must have run across the camp. "We need you both right now."

As Bryce and Cassie rushed to their feet, he realized that the moment to explain the changes in his life over the past few years was gone. But that was all right, he told himself. He'd simply explain things later. If the subject happened to come up.

They dashed across the camp to the birthing tent, Cassie and Anna struggling to keep up with Bryce's long strides.

As they entered the birthing tent, Cassie recognized the patient. Elena Hernandez lived in a village nearby. Cassie knew Elena had had several miscarriages and desperately wanted a child. She also knew that the baby was far too early, as Elena was only a little more than halfway through her third trimester.

"What's the situation?" said Bryce.

"She's fully dilated," said Anna. "But she's labored for three hours with no progress. At first I thought maybe the baby's shoulder was stuck, but it's been so long that there might be something else going on that we can't see."

Cassie was still getting used to the challenge of working without a fetal heart monitor. But as she gently ran her hands over Elena's abdomen, she had a feeling that she didn't need modern medical equipment to guess at one piece of this puzzle.

"We might be looking at twins," she said. Elena's build was slight, and Cassie surmised that malnourishment combined with premature labor was likely to make it look from the outside as though she carried one baby rather than two. She hoped there were no more than two.

"Let's cross that bridge when we come to it," said Bryce. "For now, we need to prepare for a cesarean section. We should move her to the operating tent."

In addition to working without a fetal heart monitor, there were other adjustments Cassie was making as she learned to adapt to the equipment at the medical camp. About half of the hospital beds in use had been made without wheels. In every hospital Cassie had ever worked at, she'd typically transferred patients by wheelchair or by rolling a gurney down a hall—but wheelchairs and beds with wheels were luxuries she no longer had easy access to. Transferring Elena to the operating tent's table would require some ingenuity.

Cassie watched as Bryce and Anna began unfolding a large swath of canvas. Bryce handed one end to her. She stared at it, confused.

"We're going to make a makeshift stretcher to slide her onto for transport," he explained.

Oh. Of course. Without wheels on the hospital bed or a gurney to transport Mrs. Hernandez, they'd have to be creative. Sheepishly, she grabbed one end of the canvas.

She and Bryce held the canvas taut from end to end while Anna eased Mrs. Hernandez onto it. They transported the canvas to the OR tent with small hurried steps and placed Mrs. Hernandez onto the operating table.

As they got Elena on the table, Cassie saw something that made her stomach drop. In the few minutes it had taken to transfer their patient to the operating tent, the situation had changed dramatically. Elena's abdomen had contorted into an hourglass shape, indicating that something was obstructing the birth canal. Elena was at risk of immediate uterine rupture, and possibly death, if they didn't act fast.

"Anesthetize the patient as best you can," Cassie said to the operating room nurse. "We need to start immediately. What equipment do we have available for neonatal resuscitation?"

"Just our breath and thumbs," said Bryce.

"Great," said Cassie through gritted teeth. It was life or death. If the baby was born in distress, there would be no equipment to assist—she'd have to perform neonatal CPR. If it came to that. She decided she wouldn't let it come to that.

Bryce began to make the incision for the cesarean. But inexplicably, almost as soon as he had begun, he stopped.

"What is it?" she said. "Bryce, we have to act now. There's not a moment to spare."

He handed the scalpel to her. "You do it."

"But you've already started."

"Doesn't matter. This is a complicated procedure. You should be the one to do it. You're the best ob-gyn in Brooklyn."

She took the scalpel, unwilling to quibble further while the seconds ticked away. She tried to control her intense irritation. Bryce had already started the operation. There was absolutely no reason for him to hand the scalpel over to her. What did it matter whether she or Bryce did the surgery? They were both competent doctors, and Elena and her baby needed help quickly. As she concentrated on the procedure, the thought flashed through her mind that Bryce seemed to have been *nervous* to start the C-section. But surely that couldn't be true. She'd seen Bryce deliver a few babies over the past few days, and he'd been more than competent. He was a skilled obstetrician. True, she hadn't seen him do any C-sections, but if anything, an obstetrician with Bryce's background as a surgeon should feel even *more* confident during C-sections.

But there was no time to figure out what on earth he was thinking now. Cassie carefully completed the incision. Like so many of her patients here who suffered from malnutrition, there was no fat tissue to put aside, only a thin layer of skin to protect the uterus. She made another careful incision, knowing that she had to get the baby out quickly. A clearer view showed her what had been obstructing labor: the baby's head was just a little too big. It was also a bit too far down the birth canal for her to cup and deliver.

Bryce immediately saw the problem and came to assist. With a few skilled maneuvers, Cassie was able to reach the baby's feet and deliver it bottom-first. A wave of relief washed over her as she heard the tiny cry of a newborn girl fill the room.

The others in the tent cheered as she handed the baby to one of the midwives for cleaning. She had stepped away from Elena and was letting her breath out in relief when Bryce nodded toward their patient. "Don't relax too much," he said. "You were right the first time. She had company in there."

For a moment, Cassie wasn't sure what he was talking about, but as she took another look at her patient, she saw it—the faintest flicker of motion inside the abdomen. She drew closer and saw a tiny hand.

Twins.

"I'd have missed it if it hadn't been moving just a bit," said Bryce. "You want to do the honors?"

In response, Cassie gently placed her fingers inside the abdomen, reaching for that tiny hand. She removed the second twin, a boy, and passed him to the midwife, as well.

Bryce started working on closing Elena's abdomen while two thin cries began to fill the room. For Cassie, it was the sound of victory. There would be no neonatal CPR today.

She stripped off her gloves, exhausted. Bryce gave her a huge grin and a nod. So he was impressed? Good. He should be. She was still baffled by his hesitation earlier. In a situation where every second counted, what could possibly have led Bryce to stop an emergency surgical procedure and hand the scalpel to her? She couldn't fathom what would lead him to hesitate at such a crucial moment.

She could only come to one conclusion: despite all the reports she'd heard of his daring exploits, he was just as cautious as ever. But that still didn't make sense.

Cassie knew that if she'd taken charge of the OR, she would never have stopped to question whether she or Bryce should perform the surgery. She'd simply have taken a scalpel into her hand and started, and dealt with any problems as they arose.

Then she was overcome with a wave of contrition. Despite Bryce's hesitation, they'd saved three lives that day. She smiled, knowing how much Elena had wanted to be a mother. Well, now she was, twice over.

Bryce squeezed her shoulder as he left the tent. She was determined to ask him why he'd hesitated. But before she could say more than, "Bryce, why—" he'd rushed past her.

Why would Bryce Hamlin, of all people, hesitate to do a surgery? And why did it seem as though he didn't want to talk to her about it?

CHAPTER FIVE

BRYCE SAT BENEATH his usual balsa tree, exhausted. The complicated delivery that he and Cassie had performed that morning had been the first of a day full of challenging cases, and his mind was aching for some peace. He'd worked a twelve-hour shift, but it felt like twelve years since he and Cassie had shared coffee together in the mess hall.

Now dusk was falling, and he could finally have a moment to breathe. He leaned his back against the tree's broad trunk and tried to let the tension drain from his body. The camp was surrounded on most sides by thick forest. But the trees fell away on the west side, and he could gaze at the rolling hills leading up to the mountains miles away. The sun had almost set but still cast a golden glow over the mountaintops, and underneath the balsa tree, a few early fireflies were beginning to make their appearance.

As he sat in the quiet, his stomach rumbled. He hadn't had any time to eat since breakfast. Despite the stress of the day, it had been a relief to be so busy. The rush of deliveries had meant that he hadn't been able to have a moment alone with Cassie, which meant the two of them hadn't been able to talk since that morning. He wasn't trying to avoid her, exactly. He was just certain that she'd have some questions on her mind after his noticeable hesitation during the procedure that morning, and he didn't think he was ready to answer them.

Bryce knew on an intellectual level that his tremor wasn't severe enough to prevent him from performing C-sections. Still, he was anxious whenever they were necessary. Knowing that he could do something wasn't the same thing as feeling confident about it. It was as though he'd been asked to relearn how to ride a bicycle. He could know that sitting astride a bicycle and pedaling should move him forward, but that wouldn't make him feel any more certain about keeping his balance.

Usually, if his hands started to tremble, a few deep breaths were enough to calm their twitching and allow him to continue. But this time, they hadn't stopped, and he had a feel-

ing he knew the reason why. It was because
Cassie had been there.

He wasn't sure why Cassie's presence
would affect him so much, but he thought
he could make a reasonable guess. Cassie
was the first person he'd met in El Salvador who knew the old version of himself that
he'd been in New York. When he'd first arrived in El Salvador, it had been such a relief
to finally be free of everyone's expectations.
His family, in their attempts to be support-
ive, had always spoken about what a talented
surgeon Bryce *used* to be. But in El Salvador, everyone only cared about who he was
now. He didn't have to live up to any expectations about who he'd been in the past. Instead, all he had to do was be the best doctor
he could be right now. But Cassie would expect to see the great Bryce Hamlin in action.
She would expect things to go smoothly. She
wouldn't understand if he got nervous, or if
he needed extra time with a procedure, or if
the patient's stitches didn't look like they'd
been completed by a master when he closed.

Their relationship had undergone a strange
reversal. When they'd dated, he'd been an up-
and-coming surgeon. He'd taken pride in his
talents, and his reputation was growing. He
was especially adept at maneuvers that re-

quired extra dexterity and precision. He supposed that he'd gotten used to others looking up to him. But now he found himself admiring Cassie's skills. He'd been struck by her quick action in the delivery tent, her ability to soothe Mrs. Hernandez's nerves while deftly navigating the difficult delivery. When they'd dated, she'd been a promising medical student, but she'd grown into a dedicated physician.

He, on the other hand, was no longer the star surgeon he'd been five years ago. He'd noticed her confusion as he handed her the scalpel. And he was sure she would want an explanation.

A rustling of the trees startled him for a moment, and then Cassie emerged, holding a white paper lunch bag. "Care for some company?"

He leaned his head back against the tree. "I don't know if I can be the best conversationalist right now. It's been a long day."

"I know," she said, sitting down beside him and opening the paper bag. "That's why I brought some snacks."

"Pupusas!" he cried, a smile breaking over his face. The bag contained fluffy pieces of flatbread, each stuffed with different fillings

of cheese, chicken and beans. He bit into one with gusto.

"Mmm," he said. "Chili cheese…my favorite." Only, it came out sounding like, *Hilee eese, um havorite.*

"Glad you approve. Now, I haven't been in El Salvador long, but I don't think you're supposed to eat the entire thing in one bite. At least leave yourself some room to breathe. And don't hog those. I brought them for us to share."

He slowed his chewing and passed the bag back to her. They sat on the forest floor, companionably munching their flatbread as the twilight faded.

He could only see a faint outline of her face. She sat close beside him so that she would have enough room to lean back against the balsa tree. Maybe it was because he was unable to see her face clearly, or maybe it was because of the food she'd brought him—he had been very hungry—but Bryce found himself feeling glad of her presence. Usually he preferred to be by himself after a long day. But Cassie didn't barrage him with questions or try to pull him into a conversation. Instead, they just sat together, watching the fireflies.

After they'd been silent together for a while, she said, "This is a nice spot."

"It's my favorite spot in the camp. I come here to unwind after a tough delivery, or a tough day."

"Like this morning?"

He rubbed his temples. "This morning was scary. I wasn't sure the patient was going to make it."

"But she did. They all did. There was one complication after another, but we saved three lives. I felt like I was holding my breath through the whole procedure. I still can't believe we pulled it off."

"It was mostly *you* who pulled it off," he said, wanting to give credit where it was due.

"It was a team effort, and you know it."

Well, Cassie certainly seemed to be thriving in the camp's intense atmosphere. He supposed he shouldn't be surprised. Despite how she'd changed, in many ways, she was still the Cassie he'd known five years ago. He wondered how long she would stay. Some of the camp's staff were *lifers*, returning year after year. They considered Medicine International to be their professional home. Others only joined for occasional yearlong stints. Bryce had stayed for three years, and could easily see himself staying longer. He could also see Cassie staying for a long time. To his surprise, he realized that the idea of Cassie staying at the camp for a long-term assignment held some appeal.

"It's been just over a month since you got here," he said. "Think you'll plan on sticking around for a while?"

She gave him a sidelong glance. "Trying to figure out how long you have until you'll be rid of me?"

Quite the opposite, he thought. If he were being honest with himself, he had to admit that he liked seeing her every day. But he wasn't about to tell her that. He didn't want to say anything that would lead them to revisit a host of complications.

"It's not that. It's just that it takes some people a while to adjust. You wouldn't have to deliver babies in situations like this without modern equipment back in New York."

"Are you kidding? This is exactly what I came here for. Yes, that was a stressful delivery this morning. And it was also awesome. And amazing. And incredible."

"That sounds like the Cassie I remember. You never did let a few challenges scare you off."

Even in the darkness, he could see her smile. "I'm glad to hear that you think that part of my personality hasn't changed. Before I came here, I was starting to worry that my life would be all about making sure celebrity moms got their preferred brand of organic granola, or helping some internet influencer set up cameras in the delivery room so she could livestream the moment she gave birth. But this morning was as different from my old life as I could possibly imagine. It's some of the most rewarding work I've ever done. I think I'm going to stay for a long time."

He noticed that even though her tone was casual, she seemed to be watching his face intently, trying to gauge his reaction.

Over the past few weeks, he'd grown far more comfortable with the idea of working with her than he'd been when she first arrived. He often found himself looking forward to running into her, whether it was to consult on a case or just to chat.

"I'm glad to hear you're enjoying it here," he said. "And I think…that I might be enjoying it, too."

Her eyes widened in surprise, and he quickly clarified, "I mean, I'm enjoying working together again. It's like old times."

"Old times with some new twists?"

"Exactly."

She tilted her head to one side, causing her hair to swing past her face. He often found himself wondering what it would feel like to wrap a strand of hair around one finger. He'd noticed himself banishing such thoughts from his mind more and more frequently in his attempts to respect their professional working relationship.

"I'm so glad to hear that you feel okay about working together," she said. "I was shocked to see you here, that first day, but we've done pretty well so far, haven't we?"

Her body was close enough to his that he could feel the warmth radiating from her. He mustered all of his professionalism and said, "I think so."

"And I think I figured something out this morning."

His body tensed. Had she noticed his shaking hands during the procedure?

"I finally get how you fit in to all this. Until this morning, I've been trying my hardest to solve the mystery of how cautious, mild-mannered surgeon Bryce Hamlin ended up at a medical outpost in El Salvador. But after this morning, it all makes sense. The challenges, the excitement, the adrenaline rush. How could you want to work anywhere else?"

He relaxed, relieved that she hadn't brought up his hands. "It's not always like this. Sometimes things even go pretty smoothly."

"I'll believe that when I see it. Ever since

I've gotten here, each case has had its own unique chaos."

"And you love it."

Even in the dim light, he could see that her eyes sparkled. "You know I do."

"I wouldn't expect anything less from you."

"Speaking of expectations, we didn't really get a chance to talk about your new career this morning. The last time we worked together, you were a surgeon."

"Yeah. That would be one of those new twists we were talking about."

"What happened? The Bryce I remember loved his work more than anything. But that's not the only thing that's changed. All those stories about you wrestling crocodiles, negotiating with gang members… I don't know what to make of them."

"As much as I wish the story about wrestling crocodiles were true, I'm afraid that one's the result of an overactive imagination."

"Still. You've changed. You're not a surgeon anymore. You started the C-section this morning, but then stopped and handed me the scalpel during a critical moment. You used to be obsessively protective of your hands, but now apparently you tear around on your motorcycle and jump out of helicopters without a second thought. There's something you're not telling me. Spill it."

It should have been so simple to tell her about the accident. And yet somehow, he couldn't.

He didn't want to go through explaining about the accident, everything it had taken from him and the long recovery afterward. But even more than that, he didn't want her to stop looking at him the way she was now. She seemed to think he'd grown braver and more adventurous over the years. If she knew how devastated he'd been after the accident, how it had taken away his identity, his calling, she might not look at him the same way. If she knew how he'd had to cobble a new life together out of broken pieces of his past, she might pity him. He didn't want pity from anyone, but especially not from her.

"It's true that I've been through some changes," he said. "I switched specialties. I've been living here in El Salvador for three years, and I suppose that would change anyone. But does it really matter why? Maybe I just needed something different, like you did."

"It matters if it's my fault."

"Your fault? What are you talking about?"

"You lost your fellowship because of me."

Now he remembered. The Beaumont Fellowship. Weeks before the accident, he'd learned he had been removed from consideration for the fellowship because he was on probation. At the time, the news had been terribly disappointing. But then being hit by a drunk driver several weeks later had put things in perspective.

But Cassie hadn't known about the accident. And now she sounded absolutely wretched. She felt guilty, he realized. She thought that his change of careers had something to do with her.

"First of all, I lost the fellowship because I was on probation," he said. "And I was on probation because of a decision that we made, together. And even though the hospital administrators disagreed, I still think we made the right decision."

"But starting the operation was my idea. If I hadn't convinced you, you never would have followed through with it."

It was true that when they'd dated, he'd been known for being cautious, always leaning toward the safest option. Had she thought that just because he was reserved he didn't have a mind of his own?

"That's simply not true. Despite what you may believe, it is possible to stand up to Cassie Andover. The final judgment call was mine, and I'd make the same call again today. So I'm not sure why you're feeling so guilty about it."

"Because I got off so lightly!" she cried. "They blamed you for everything. I should have been suspended at the very least. But instead, I got a stern warning and a talking-to, and before I knew it everything was back to normal. I worked so hard to repair my reputation. In fact, I worked too hard. I gave up everything that made me feel like myself, because I didn't like who I was. I don't deserve to be known as the best obstetrician in New York. I don't deserve any of it. I didn't deserve you."

He could see that tears were streaming quietly down her face. He put his arm around her, rather gingerly at first, but then he held her closer. The whole time he was recovering from the accident, he'd known nothing about the guilt Cassie was holding on to. How could he?

As he held Cassie, he wondered if he should have handled things differently. He'd told himself that his anger and hurt over the way she'd left had prevented him from trying to reach out to her, to talk things over, but now he wondered if his own pride had gotten in his way.

She's the one who left me, his anger had retorted. He'd spent years clinging to that anger, painting himself as the victim in their breakup because anger was easier to deal with than pain.

Except it was one thing to blame her for the breakup from afar. But now, holding her in his arms in the darkness while she cried, somehow it didn't seem to matter whose fault the breakup had been. All that mattered was that it was in the past. Here, in the present, he just didn't want Cassie to hurt anymore.

"I had no idea you felt this way," he said. "But for what it's worth, you are not the reason I stopped being a surgeon. And when I finally did stop, it was freeing. It opened up a whole new world for me that I never would have considered otherwise."

"Really?" she said, drying her eyes on the sleeve of her coat.

He hesitated. He'd meant to tell a small white lie designed to make Cassie feel better. After the accident, nothing had felt freeing at all. He'd been heartbroken when he realized that no matter how much work he put into physical therapy, his hands were never going to be steady enough to be a surgeon's hands again. But if he told Cassie about the accident now, it would only add to her guilt.

And so he told her a different part of the story, a part that was mostly true, even if it left out the accident and all the fallout from it.

"You know how you said your parents were overprotective? Well, mine were just as bad."

She laughed through the last traces of her tears. "I'm not sure that's possible."

"Okay, maybe mine weren't quite as bad as yours. I was never forbidden from riding my bicycle or going to the playground. But both my parents were trauma surgeons. They would come home from work and scare my sister and I with stories of patients who'd hurt themselves by doing things that were dangerous or careless. I think their intentions were good. They were trying to get us to think and be cautious. But they may have gone a little overboard."

"It sounds like my parents would approve of their methods. Maybe we should get them all in a room together so they can exchange child-rearing tips." She shuddered. "Actually, that's probably a terrible idea."

He couldn't help smiling. "Let's make sure they never meet. You'd think they would have become more relaxed after I became a surgeon, but instead, they got worse. They were always warning me to protect my hands at all costs. My hands were my career, they always said."

"No wonder you were always so obsessive about hand injuries."

"I know. I didn't have a rebellious phase like you did. Surgery was kind of my thrill. It was life-and-death enough for me."

"But then why would you ever stop?"

"I guess after we broke up… I realized I needed to find out who I was. All of my plans for my life have always been wrapped up in other people. My career was what it was because I came from a family of surgeons. I never had a chance to consider anything else." He swallowed.

"Anyway, I realized I was living a life based on other people's hopes and dreams for me," he continued. "And other people's worries, too. All those stories my parents told about patients who'd been horribly injured in accidents, all of my father's lectures about protecting my hands, because God forbid I should twist a finger and not be able to perform surgery for a few weeks… All of it made me way too cautious. It kept me from living my real life."

She nodded slowly. "You needed to get

away from everyone else's expectations in order to find yourself."

He was surprised to find that her words seemed so exactly right, even though he hadn't shared the whole truth with her. Even though he'd never wanted to give up surgery, life *had* become more exciting after his surgical career was over. He'd never needed to seek out excitement before, because surgery had been exciting enough. But without having it in his life, he'd had to open himself up to new things, sometimes taking new risks. It had been freeing after all, he realized, to give up surgery and all the pressure of it, and find a whole new side of himself in El Salvador.

She shook her head slowly. "All this time, I was blaming myself for putting your career at risk."

"I hope you don't feel guilty anymore," he said, meaning it. As he spoke, he realized that he himself didn't feel angry anymore. It was strange, he thought, that after harboring that anger for so long, it could simply drift away. Yet as he saw Cassie's face, half lit in the shadows, he knew that he never wanted her to feel guilty when she thought about him. And he didn't want to be angry with her.

In fact, when he looked at her now, he felt an entirely different range of emotions. He wondered if she could ever possibly feel the same about him.

She blotted her eyes with her sleeve. He knew he should take his arm from around her shoulders, but he couldn't bring himself to do it.

"Just think," he said. "If I were still a surgeon, I wouldn't have been there today to watch the best ob-gyn in New York help a mom from a rural mountain village in El Salvador bring her twins into the world. I wouldn't have been here to help save three lives."

"Thanks," she said. "I'm glad that our ability to work together hasn't changed. And I think I'm actually glad that we're both here together."

"And I'm glad you're no longer horrified at the thought of working with me."

"Oh, it was never horrifying. Just very, very surprising. It's funny… I came here because I thought I needed to get away from my past, but I never thought I needed this."

"Needed what?" he asked.

"To see you again."

She looked up at him. They were enveloped in shadow, and yet the moon was bright enough that he could see her face. Her eyes were still wet with the last drops of tears, and they shimmered in the moonlight. On impulse, he reached a finger to her cheek and brushed a single tear away.

As he felt her skin beneath his fingertips, he realized that this was the first time he'd touched her since the day she'd arrived at the camp.

He rested his hand against her cheek for a moment longer than he meant to. Her hair brushed his fingertips and he was gripped by an irrational desire to smooth the stray locks around her forehead.

She held his gaze, and he realized their faces were only inches apart.

He knew he should move away, as much as he didn't want to.

He mustered every last bit of resolve he could find and started to pull away from her. But as he started to pull back and began to say, "I'm sorry," she leaned in and stopped his words with a light kiss. And then both his arms were around her and he was holding her even tighter, close to his chest. Their lips met again, not lightly at all this time, but a deep kiss in which his mouth pressed against hers, demanding entry, pouring five years of yearning into a single moment. Her mouth yielded readily to his, inviting him to revisit familiar ground and to explore new territory.

There was a new taste of wild berries, but underneath it the familiar taste of sweetness and *her*. As her lips opened beneath his, he found he could no longer discern what was familiar and what was new, because he was lost in the heat and warmth of Cassie as he crushed his lips against hers.

As he leaned in closer, pressing her back against the tree trunk, she made a small squeak. He broke away from her instantly.

"It's just…the trunk was poking into my back," she said.

And just as abruptly as it had begun, the moment was over.

He felt thoroughly embarrassed. He couldn't believe he'd allowed himself to get so caught up in the moment that he'd kissed her.

He could still taste the faint sweetness of berries on his lips.

He was playing with fire, and he knew it. He'd already been hurt by Cassie once before. He'd assumed she wanted more of a life together than she did, and he'd paid the price for that assumption. He had no idea, now, what she wanted out of a relationship, but five years ago, he'd had the experience of being one of her thrills, easily disposed of. He didn't want to put himself through that again, no matter how much he wanted to continue holding her in his arms.

And so he disentangled himself from her and stood, brushing himself off. She stood, too.

"I'm sorry," he said, just as she blurted out the same words.

"It's okay," she said. "I know you want to keep things professional."

"Right," he said. "I think with all this talk of old memories, and with it being such a long day for both of us, maybe we both got a little bit tired and…confused."

"Of course," she said. "It's been a very long day. I'm sure once we both get some sleep, we can start over again in the morning."

"Nothing would make me happier."

"Well, then. We're agreed. I think it's long past time I went back to my quarters and got some sleep. Hand me that last *pupusa* for the road?"

He gave her the flatbread and watched her retreat into the darkness.

He told himself that he was glad he'd stopped the kiss when he did. But he noticed that he had to work awfully hard to convince himself that *not* kissing her could ever be the right thing.

And yet, he'd been hurt by Cassie in the

past, and he knew what that felt like. He wasn't interested in something that would turn out to be just another meaningless fling to her. He was tired of wasting time on heartbreak, and if he were to get involved with anyone again, he would want that person to be looking for a serious future. But he had no idea if that's what Cassie was looking for, and he'd been wrong once before. Getting involved with Cassie again would be moving backward, and if there was one thing Bryce had learned over the past five years, it was how to move forward, even if the circumstances weren't ideal. Even if he cared for someone who didn't feel the same way about him.

Cassie went back to her quarters, but she failed to get any sleep. Instead, she gazed up at the mosquito netting that protected her bed, replaying the moments that had led up to the kiss over and over in her mind.

She could still feel the warmth and pressure of where he'd held her on her body. It had felt every bit as good to be wrapped in those arms as she'd imagined.

She hadn't expected the kiss to happen. And yet when it did, it felt so right. Like coming home.

When Bryce explained that she wasn't at fault for his career change, she'd felt so relieved. She'd meant what she said: she *had* needed to see him again. All this time, she'd thought she needed to stay away from him as much as possible. But now, knowing that Bryce had found it freeing to give up surgery, knowing that he'd dealt with high expectations and overprotectiveness from his parents, just as she had, made all the difference.

With a pang, she wondered if they could have talked about all of this five years ago. But there was no use looking back. Five years ago, Bryce hadn't given up surgery, and she hadn't given up blaming herself for all his troubles. But now it seemed that Bryce had never blamed her at all...and apparently there was no reason for her to blame herself.

But if he'd forgiven her, why had he been so brusque after the kiss?

Just because he'd forgiven her didn't mean he wanted her. Maybe he'd merely been feeling nostalgic. He'd essentially said as much. *I think with all this talk of old memories, and with it being such a long day for both of us, maybe we both got a little bit tired and...confused.*

So he'd been *confused* when he kissed her. And yet during the kiss, he hadn't seemed confused at all. She shivered, remembering his arms pressing her to his chest, the masculine warmth of his lips on hers. Far from confused, he'd seemed to know exactly what he wanted, for a moment.

But just for a moment. As soon as they'd broken apart, he'd become businesslike. Still, for all their talk of staying professional, Bryce hadn't kissed her as though he wanted to stay professional. He'd kissed her as though he meant it. As though he wanted more.

It amazed her how their kiss had felt so natural, but seconds later they'd been so awkward with one another. She wished she knew how Bryce really felt. Did he think the kiss was a mistake or had he simply been caught up in the heat of the moment?

Or perhaps, just possibly, the kiss meant something…more.

She'd practically fled the scene afterward, afraid that she might say something terribly wrong and completely botch the moment. Or that she'd hear him say more about being— she rolled her eyes—*confused.*

She hadn't wanted to stop the kiss, but she wondered if Bryce had felt as though he had to. Five years ago, he thought she had left him without a care in the world. He'd never realized how guilty she felt. Or just how hard it had been for her to leave. He still didn't realize all that he had meant to her.

She wondered if there was any way to show him just how wrong he was about that.

So much had changed since they'd last known each other. She'd almost lost her adventurous side forever, and he'd almost gotten engaged. He'd done what people were supposed to do after breakups: try to move on. She just wished that he hadn't gone through it all believing that he was nothing more than a fling to her.

After everything that had passed between the two of them, the chances of she and Bryce becoming anything more than friends to one another were smaller than the tiny mosquitoes trapped in the netting above her bed.

Which was a problem. Because she refused to accept that that kiss under the balsa tree was the last kiss she would share with Bryce.

Somehow, she was going to show him that their relationship wasn't just a thrill to her, and never had been. She just needed to think of a way to do it.

CHAPTER SIX

OVER THE NEXT few days, the medical camp was busier than Cassie had ever seen it. A series of landslides in the mountains had displaced the residents of a number of rural villages, and more families were arriving at the camp every day.

The extra work meant that she had barely any time to herself, let alone to speak with Bryce. As desperate as she was to speak with him, she also felt nervous about what she would learn if she did.

After their talk under the balsa tree, it was nice to feel as though they were friends again. But as Cassie considered their kiss, she was faced with a growing realization that friendship wasn't going to be enough. She wanted more. Much more.

And there was no time to find out whether Bryce felt the same way.

She couldn't stop thinking about the kiss.

Her sleep was terrible, to the point where one of the midwives commented on the dark circles under her eyes. Cassie had gotten flustered and said something about the long shifts getting to her. She hadn't wanted to admit that each night she fought for sleep but was kept awake by the memory of Bryce's lips on hers. And, of course, thinking about that led to all the other memories she had of times when Bryce's lips had been on hers. And that left her wanting more.

She tried to tell herself that there were countless reasons she should let all of the memories go, including the memory of their most recent kiss. She ticked the reasons off in her mind. They'd agreed to be professional. Bryce had probably only kissed her out of nostalgia. It would probably be incredibly hard for him to trust his heart with her again.

She wanted so badly to show him that he could. But she didn't know how. She didn't even know if Bryce felt anything more than friendship for her.

But as the days passed, she couldn't deny that she wanted more than friendship from him.

At first, she tried to cope with her feelings by ignoring them. She threw herself into her work, just as she had in New York. Back then, she'd been trying to forget that Bryce existed.

Now, she was trying to forget how his kiss had made her feel. As well as the jolt of electricity she felt when his arm brushed against hers in passing. And the flutter of butterfly wings in her stomach when she caught him glancing in her direction.

Her strategy was about as effective now as it had been back then. Which was to say, not very effective at all.

When she'd first arrived at the camp, it had been hard enough adjusting to seeing Bryce every day while she worked. Now she had to deal with seeing him every time she closed her eyes in her quarters at night.

Despite her fears about what Bryce might say, she knew they needed a chance to speak alone. She had to know how he felt.

Especially because there were moments where she could swear she'd caught Bryce staring at her. His glances were discreet, but they were definitely there. And they were intense enough to make her wonder if he was thinking about their kiss under the balsa tree every bit as much as she was. And perhaps experiencing some rekindled desire of his own.

But she couldn't know unless they talked.

And as each day at the camp became busier than the last, she wasn't sure when she'd be able to speak with him.

Then, inspiration struck. She'd been reviewing patient charts and listening to little Manny chatter away about a jaguar with cubs that he and Bryce had supposedly come upon in the forest when Bryce took him along on a medical mission. Manny's story reminded her that Bryce and some of the other doctors went on medical missions all the time. Usually they delivered vaccines, transported refugees away from dangerous mountain areas vulnerable to volcanic eruptions and rockfalls or helped with difficult births when women couldn't reach the camp. Cassie had been hoping for a chance to join such a mission herself as soon as she could, but she'd been absorbed in adjusting to life at the camp.

Now, she realized that joining a mission might be the perfect opportunity to get some alone time with Bryce. Enrique had told her that Bryce did most of the off-camp missions. He'd said that he often wanted to send another doctor along with Bryce for backup, but the camp lacked the manpower.

Cassie was more than eager to help. The camp was so busy that it was the only way that she and Bryce would ever be able to get some time to themselves. Hopefully, they'd have a chance to talk about what was going on between the two of them.

Even if he only wanted to be friends, she needed to know. Because nothing was worse than not knowing if he would ever kiss her like that again.

As she'd predicted, Enrique was thrilled when she volunteered to be available for any upcoming off-camp missions.

"It'll be good to have more people who can go off-camp besides Bryce, especially because it's best to send people in pairs," he'd said. "I'll keep you in mind for the next mission that comes up."

But as the days passed, nothing out of the ordinary happened, other than one of the camp's rickety wooden shower stall doors falling in on her as she rinsed her hair.

She took her showers early in the morning, for both the hot water and the privacy. For the most part, she was impressed with how well the camp managed to provide protection from the elements in the middle of the wilderness. The cinder block buildings and canvas tents might not be pleasing to the eye, but they were safe and sterile. But the showers left much to be desired. They were relics of an earlier era, the only buildings in the camp made of wood rather than concrete. The showerheads were little more than hoses jury-rigged to the walls so that water cascaded from above. The wood doors almost hung off their posts, and extreme care had to be taken to make sure they didn't come apart upon opening or closing.

I just wanted some excitement, she thought, grumpily making her way from the shower stall back to her quarters. *I didn't think that would involve taking my own life in my hands every time I shower.*

She was still muttering under her breath in frustration a few minutes later, after she'd thrown on a khaki field shirt and made her way to the mess hall for her morning coffee. Enrique and Bryce were already there, and Cassie forgot her frustration as she heard their conversation.

"It shouldn't take more than a couple of days," she heard Enrique saying. "I don't want to take you away from your patients, but the farthest town is only a day's drive from camp."

As she approached, both men turned toward her, and Enrique said, "Ah, Cassie! Just the person I'd hoped to see!"

"Why's that?" said Cassie and Bryce at

once, and Cassie noticed that Bryce's tone had a suspicious edge.

"I need two doctors to deliver a load of vaccines to Juayua and to a couple of other towns outside the camp."

"Why-*what*-a?" she asked.

"Why-*yoo*-wah," he enunciated. "Juayua. It's a lovely town."

"Now wait a minute," said Bryce. "I thought that you and I were going to go."

Enrique bit his lip with apprehension. "That's why I was hoping to see you, Cassie. Originally, the plan was for Bryce and me to make the trip together. But I have the chance to start some furlough a little bit earlier than planned if I leave tomorrow. I know it's short notice, but if you go, I can spend a couple of extra days with my wife in San Salvador."

"Of course!" she said at once. "I've wanted to see more of the countryside, and I'm happy to help you out."

Bryce's frown deepened. "Cassie's only been here for a few weeks. She's not ready for a field mission."

Cassie opened her mouth to protest, but Enrique was already rolling his eyes at Bryce. "Don't listen to him," he said to Cassie. "You've been here for over a month—just as long as Bryce, when he started accompanying me on missions. Of course, I'd never ask you to go if you were uncomfortable."

"Not at all," she said, ignoring Bryce's scowl.

"Excellent. It's more than a matter of simply dropping off the meds at each village. You'll need to do brief demonstrations of how and when to administer each one, and spend some time explaining what the vaccines will do. Some of them are antimalarial, so you'll need to make it especially clear which ones are safe for pregnant mothers and which are not."

"Count me in," she said.

"Shouldn't Cassie have at least a few months to settle in before you start sending her tearing off through the countryside?"

"Oh, come on," said Enrique. "A trip to Juayua isn't exactly the same as trip through gang territory up in the mountains. In fact, it'd be a great way to introduce her to the wider world of El Salvador." He turned toward Cassie. "If you go, you're in for a treat. The road you'd be traveling is one of our most famous—it's called the Ruta de Las Flores, because of all the wildflowers that grow like a carpet on either side of the highway. It's definitely one of the most beautiful parts of the country. There are tons of places to stop for the best coffee you've ever had along the way, as well as some lovely murals to take in at each town. And there are some beautiful hiking areas and waterfalls around Juayua. The trip will take at least two days, and your first furlough won't be coming up for a while, so you should take advantage of it."

"Cassie should stay in the camp, where it's safe," Bryce said.

Cassie bristled. Bryce's caution brought out the familiar urge to rebel. She knew that El Salvador had its dangers, but she hardly blinked at the idea of leaving the safe familiarity of the camp. She had a feeling that she knew what was really bothering Bryce. They hadn't been alone together since their kiss, and now they were about to go on an overnight mission—that she'd had a minor hand in orchestrating. But he didn't need to know that.

"Bryce," she said calmly. "Might I have a word with you, for a second?"

She pulled him aside from Enrique. "Look, just be honest with me. Should we talk about why you don't want me going on this mission with you?"

"I already explained. You're still adjusting to life here."

"Would you be putting up this much of a

fight if any of our other coworkers wanted to go with you?"

"No," he admitted. "But no one else here knows you like I do. And I was also trying to give you a way out, in case you didn't want to go with me, after what happened a few nights ago."

She was relieved that his reluctance seemed to stem from his desire to make sure she felt comfortable. She wondered if his avoidance of her lately had been because he thought she was the one who didn't want to talk. At least it wasn't that he didn't want her company on the mission.

"I'm excited to go," she said. "I really am. Look, we both agreed to be professional, and the two of us going on missions together is going to have to be part of that."

He nodded, conceding her point. They turned back to Enrique.

"All right," Bryce said. "We'll head out first thing tomorrow."

"Great!" said Enrique. "That means I can leave tomorrow to meet my wife in San Salvador. She'll be thrilled that I have an extra day of furlough. I can't tell you how much I appreciate this, Cassie." He clapped a frowning Bryce on the shoulder. "And I'm going to need the milk truck, so you'll be able to take that blasted motorcycle of yours instead. That should cheer you up."

Bryce still looked somewhat reluctant. "Be ready at dawn tomorrow," he said to Cassie. "We'll need to be on the road before 6:00 a.m."

Bryce kicked the large boulder that marked the entrance to Enrique's administrative tent. Immediately, his foot began to throb. The boulder, for its part, remained unaffected.

He wasn't frustrated because he didn't want Cassie to come with him to Juayua. He was frustrated because he wasn't sure he'd be able to handle an overnight trip with Cassie.

He'd already shown that he couldn't trust himself to control his feelings when he'd kissed Cassie several days ago. How the hell was he going to get through an overnight trip alone with her?

His attraction to her was just an attraction, and nothing more.

But despite his intentions, he kept thinking about that kiss. How good it had felt, and if there might be some way to make it happen again. Since he couldn't keep his mind off those thoughts, trying to keep his distance from Cassie was the least he could do.

He decided that this was all Enrique's fault.

Why had he specifically asked Cassie to take his place on the mission?

"What the hell was that all about?" he asked his boss, who looked back at him with wide-eyed innocence.

"I'm not sure what you mean."

"That whole thing back there, pressuring Cassie into venturing outside camp before she's ready!"

"Pressuring her? If you must know, she asked to be put on a few off-camp missions. I thought she was ready, and I knew she was interested, so I wanted to ask her to take my place."

This was news. He hadn't realized that Cassie had volunteered for any missions. For a moment, he wondered if she'd volunteered because she knew that he did most of the off-camp missions, and she wanted a chance to be alone with him. But then he remembered who he was thinking about. Cassie had always had a thirst for adventure. He was part of the adventure this time.

"I thought she seemed pretty eager to go," Enrique continued. "If anything, you were pressuring her to stay at the camp. Do you honestly think she'll be in danger on the Ruta de Las Flores? Especially with you there? She'll be fine. You'll both be fine. Personally, I thought that sending Cassie out on a mission in one of the more serene parts of the country would be a good way to get her feet wet."

"Did you? Because it sounded an awful lot more like you were setting us up on a date."

Enrique raised his eyebrows. "I was merely trying to describe the situation accurately."

Bryce snorted. "Really. *Tons of coffee places to stop at?* A *carpet* of wildflowers?"

Enrique shrugged. "I can't help that the road happens to be very beautiful."

"And what's this about you needing the milk truck all of a sudden?"

"I need it to run a few errands on my way to San Salvador. I have to say, I'm surprised by your reaction. I did think you'd be thrilled. I thought you'd be here in my tent saying, *Thank you, boss, for sending me on an easy mission through one of the loveliest parts of the country.* And yet somehow it seems to me that you aren't pleased." He paused thoughtfully. "It seems to me that it's not exactly the mission but the company that concerns you. I get the impression that there's more to your relationship with Cassie than you've let on?"

"We used to date."

"I knew it! Dr. Andover is a delightful, intelligent, beautiful woman—so of *course* you dated. Did you screw it up? Do I need to move you two to separate schedules? Wait, you're not going to transfer, are you? You can't leave, Bryce. We need you here."

"No, no." Bryce waved his hands. "We don't hate each other at all. We're fine. Nobody's transferring. And I didn't screw it up—she left me, if you must know, although I'd rather not get into all of it. It was a long time ago, and it's…complicated."

"With you, my friend, it always is."

"I'm just saying that while it's been fine working with Cassie… I'm not sure about going on a trip together."

"Because?"

Bryce hesitated, and Enrique said, "Oh, I get it. You still have feelings for her."

"Absolutely not. That's in the past, and even if it were true, it wouldn't matter, because she just wants friendship."

"Uh-huh. So does your *friend* know that you still have feelings for her?"

"Enrique. All of that was over a long time ago."

"Exactly! You've both had a long time to change. Maybe her feelings toward you have changed, too. She wanted to go on this trip with you, didn't she?"

"That doesn't mean anything. Cassie's always loved a thrill. She's probably just bored with the camp and wants a little excitement."

"And this is the perfect time for you to offer her exactly that!"

"That was the problem before. She liked to get swept up in the thrill. And that's all I was to her—a thrill. We dated back in my surgery days…back when I was the up-and-coming superstar who was always asked to scrub in on the complex cases. She and I weren't even supposed to date, because I was a resident and she was a med student. But after it was all over, I realized that that was the appeal for her. It wasn't me she liked. It was that she was secretly dating the superstar surgeon. That's who she was attracted to."

"Hmm. Maybe. But have you ever thought that it might have been *you* who was attracted to the superstar surgeon?"

"Excuse me?"

"Being a surgeon fit all your dreams, and your family's dreams. And you were good at it. You got a lot of recognition for a talent that you had. You got to be a superstar. But did you ever spend time just being plain old Bryce?"

Bryce thought for a moment. "Not until after the accident. Even then, everyone seemed more interested in the memory of who I used to be, rather than who I'd become. I don't think I felt like myself again until I came here."

"Exactly. Most people start out as plain old versions of themselves, and have to work to become a star. You started out a star, and now you have to be okay with being just the regular you. Fortunately for everyone here, the regular you is the person this camp needs. There are no rock star surgeons here. Just good docs who do good work. And who are willing to tame jaguars once in a while."

Bryce chuckled. "Manny again. That kid."

"He says you have a pet jaguar in a cave in the forest."

"Hmm, I'll bet that's his excuse for sneaking extra snack rations—that he needs to go and feed it."

Enrique grew thoughtful. "So you and Cassie dated back when you were a surgeon. But when she first arrived here at the camp, she asked me why you'd changed your specialty to obstetrics. She doesn't know about the accident, does she? She doesn't know that you quit surgery because of the tremor in your hands."

Bryce rubbed the back of his neck. "The accident happened so soon after the breakup. I wasn't ready to talk to her. And most of all—" he swallowed, trying to keep his voice steady "—I didn't want her pity."

"Okay, but why not just tell her about it now?"

Bryce sighed. "Growing up in a family full of surgeons I used to be completely overcautious about my hands, with myself. She was always so…fearless. And now she's hearing about me going on all the missions here, and I can tell she sees me differently. I want her to think I've actually changed. Not that I was just some…victim of circumstance. I want her to think that I really have become braver."

"But haven't you? Last I checked, you do like motorcycles, and probably roller coasters, too. It seems to me that the person she believes you are is…you."

"Yes…but I like that she sees me as someone who changed because he… I don't know, grew as a person, I guess. Not someone who was a victim of an unfortunate accident and had to change his life because it was the only way to move forward."

Enrique let out a low whistle as he shook his head. "Yeah, you *definitely* don't have feelings for her. None at all."

"Look, even if I did have feelings, they would just make things more complicated. So it's best to just leave things alone."

"Great idea. Let me know how that goes. Meantime, I'm going to go video chat with my wife. For some reason, hearing all this from you has made me especially appreciative to have the love of a good woman."

The next morning, Cassie woke just before dawn, flushed with excitement at the prospect of seeing more of El Salvador. She dressed hastily, remembering Bryce's request that they leave as early as possible. As she threw a spare set of clothes and other necessities into a small backpack, she realized that she was about to spend two days with someone who she'd once thought was out of her life forever. Just six weeks ago, if someone had told her she'd be working with Bryce Hamlin again, she wouldn't have believed it.

It was amazing how dramatically things could change in such a short amount of time. She'd never thought she would see Bryce again, let alone become friends with him. Yet here they were, going on a medical mission together.

Maybe, she thought, this could be her chance to prove that she had valued their relationship. That he'd meant more to her back then than he realized. And now…she wasn't sure if there was any possibility of things going beyond friendship. But if there was any hope of Bryce kissing her again the way he had the other night, he'd need to know that she had never meant to hurt him.

She stepped out of her quarters to see Bryce waiting just outside, strapping a cargo box to the back of his motorcycle. Little Manny was helping, running back and forth for various items for Bryce to add to his storage compartment.

"So we're taking the bike?" she said, barely able to hide the excitement in her voice. Her heart lifted at the idea of taking to the open road.

"Don't worry," he said, mistaking the excitement in her voice for apprehension. "I've given it a thorough tune-up since our last excursion. It's not going to break down this time. And the road we'll be on is well-traveled, so we're unlikely to hit any rocks or roots like we did before."

Far from worried, she was thrilled. She'd been dying for a chance to get back on that motorcycle since her first day in El Salvador.

"Can't I come?" Manny begged. "I could fit right on top of the cargo box. Please, please, please?"

"Not this time," said Bryce. "It's too far away, and even the safer parts of El Salvador

aren't exactly safe. It's certainly too dangerous for a kid."

Manny looked crestfallen. Cassie thought
she knew how the boy felt; after all, she'd
spent most of her childhood surrounded
by adults who told her that everything she
wanted to do was too dangerous.

"It's also too much time to spend away
from your family," she told the boy. "You
have a baby sister to look after. Where would
she be without her big brother? You stay here
and protect Rosibel, keep her safe until we
get back."

Manny gave a begrudging nod, indicating
that for the sake of his sister's welfare, he was
willing to forego an adventure with Bryce.

Bryce switched on the ignition, and as
Cassie eased her body onto the bike behind
him, she couldn't help feel her heart begin to
soar. She put her arms around Bryce's waist
and nodded when he asked if she was ready.

Once again, he held out his leather jacket to
her. She did a small internal fist pump of excitement as she put it on. She hadn't thought
she'd get to wear the jacket again. But, of
course, she didn't have one of her own, and
Bryce wouldn't want her to go unprotected.

She wrapped her arms around his torso,

noticing once again how firm his body had become.

You're on a medical mission, remember? she thought. *Try to maintain some self-control.*

She nuzzled her nose into the collar to smell the warm spicy notes of Bryce's jacket. Self-control wasn't going to be easy. But she'd never backed away from a challenge. Bryce had said so the other night. Just a few moments before he'd kissed her.

She held on tight as the bike took off with a thundering roar.

CHAPTER SEVEN

IT FELT AMAZING to be back on a motorcycle again.

Cassie's trip with Bryce several weeks ago, when she'd first arrived in El Salvador, had given her just a small taste of how much she'd missed the freedom of the road. More than that, she'd missed the sense of glorious possibility that accompanied the sensation of speeding along stretches of wide-open highway. The feeling of adventure was intoxicating.

The road was every bit as beautiful as it was rumored to be. They were driving along the Ruta de las Flores—the Road of Flowers—and Cassie could see that it was aptly named. The roadside was thick with purple, pink and yellow wildflowers. In the distance, a volcanic mountain range towered over the horizon. Cassie knew that many of El Salvador's volcanoes were active, but the peaks of the range were unexpectedly lush and green, contrasting nicely with the blue of a cloudless sky. As the miles of road dropped away behind them, Cassie felt the sensation of flying, as though she were a bird skimming the road with its wings.

She chalked up most of her excitement to the thrill of being back on a motorcycle.

But as amazing as it was to be back on a motorcycle, it was even more amazing to be next to Bryce again.

His jacket enveloped her in his scent, just as it had on their earlier ride. She knew he'd only lent it to her because it was in his nature to be protective. But sitting behind him, with her arms wrapped around his torso and the warmth of his body close to hers, it was hard not to get swept up in the emotions that washed over her.

She felt tears forming at the corners of her eyes that had nothing to do with the wind. It had been far too long since she'd had such a sensation of pure joy, she thought. Overworked and burned-out, she hadn't realized how long it had been since she'd simply let herself enjoy the moment. Whatever this feeling was, she didn't want to let go of it ever again. She let out a whoop, unable to stop herself, and not caring whether Bryce heard.

But he must have, because at her cry, he went even faster, and she let out another shout of delight. This, she thought, was how life was meant to be.

They rode steadily for most of the morning. The road wound through coffee plantations and towns with brightly colored houses, where they stopped every so often for breaks. The plan, Bryce explained, was to stop at three different towns to give vaccines and educational presentations to the residents, and then spend the night in Juayua before returning the next day.

Their first stop was Apaneca, where Cassie was charmed by the cobbled streets and adobe houses. After they'd delivered a batch of vaccines, they stopped for coffee at a small roadside shop. One wall of the shop had been painted with an elaborate mural of flowers and butterflies, and Cassie and Bryce sat outside, sipping their coffee and discussing their plan of attack for the next two towns. A lifelong caffeine addict, Cassie considered herself something of a connoisseur when it came to coffee. El Salvadoran blends were fuller and bolder than she was used to, with a somewhat floral aroma. She inhaled deeply, savoring the scent.

Bryce was drinking coffee, too, but he

seemed to be drinking it rather hastily, and Cassie noticed that he kept looking at his watch.

"Slow down!" she protested as he finished his remaining coffee in one big gulp. "It's a crime to drink coffee this good so fast!"

"You think this coffee is good? Well, just wait until we get to Juayua. The coffee there puts this stuff to shame."

"Nonsense. This is one of the best cups of coffee I've ever had. Why are you really hurrying?"

"Well. Here's the thing. Every weekend there's a food festival in Juayua, called the Feria Gastronomica."

"Hmm, a food festival. Why do I suddenly have the feeling that we're not just on this trip to deliver vaccines?"

Bryce checked his watch again. "If we make it quick, we can wrap things up in Salcoatitán in about an hour, and then hit Juayua by early afternoon. Just in time to have some of the best street food El Salvador has to offer."

She cocked an eyebrow at him. "You just might be speaking the language of my heart, Bryce Hamlin. What kind of food are we talking about?"

"Everything under the sun, and trust me, it's all delicious."

"I don't know, Bryce. You are asking me to rush through a pretty damn good cup of coffee just on faith alone."

"I promise it's worth it. I make a trip to drop off medical supplies to Juayua every few months, and the food festival's the main reason I always volunteer to make the run."

She gasped in mock indignation. "Wait a minute. This festival's the *main* reason? What about your passion for providing medical care? What about building ties among the communities we serve?"

"Those are all nice perks, but the real reason I got into this doctoring business was so I could indulge in local cuisine."

Cassie drank the rest of her own coffee in a final gulp. "Then it sounds like we'd better get a move on."

His eyes danced. "There's the Cassie I remember. Always up for new things."

She smiled at his enthusiasm. Where had this carefree version of Bryce been when they were dating? Five years ago, if they'd gone on a trip like this together, she'd have expected him to maintain their schedule with meticulous care. And he'd have driven something much more practical than a motorcycle. But now, he seemed relaxed. He even seemed as though he were having fun.

She'd never known he could be like this. But then, clearly, she hadn't known him as well as she'd thought.

A short time later, they arrived at the town of Salcoatitán, where they demonstrated how to administer the vaccines to town officials in a beautiful nineteenth-century church. Before getting back onto the road, they stretched their legs under a giant tree that loomed over the town square.

"Couldn't we just stay here for the rest of the day and do Juayua tomorrow?" she asked, stretching her arms overhead. The afternoon sunlight was luxurious, and she was beginning to feel sleepy.

"Nope," he said firmly. "The food festival's only on weekends, so we have to keep to a tight schedule. It'll be worth it, I promise."

She gave him a skeptical look.

"All right, here's something I know you won't be able to resist. There's a huge waterfall that's about a twenty-minute hike outside Juayua."

A waterfall? Her eyes gleamed. She'd been aching to see a waterfall since the day she arrived.

"Let's get a move on," she said, snapping

her helmet back on. "We don't want to stand around here and lose the rest of the day."

It was midafternoon when they finally arrived in Juayua. They were greeted enthusiastically by a woman with a kind face and graying hair. Bryce introduced the woman as Gina Lopez, one of the town's most senior midwives and their medical liaison to the local health community.

"Mrs. Lopez is one of the best midwives in the country," said Bryce. "We'd get nowhere in Juayua without her."

"Nonsense," said Mrs. Lopez, giving Bryce a fond smile. "I've birthed most of the babies in this town. But every so often there's something that's more than what a midwife can handle. There are mothers and children who wouldn't be here today if there weren't a Medicine International outpost within driving distance."

They discussed the vaccines with Mrs. Lopez, and she invited them to stay for dinner. "Not this time," said Bryce. "It's Cassie's first time in Juayua, and she was really hoping to go to the Feria Gastronomica."

Cassie rolled her eyes. "*I* was really hoping to go?" she muttered to Bryce as Mrs. Lopez led them back outside.

"You haven't lived until you've had the prawn sticks," he muttered back.

Outside the house, Mrs. Lopez's teenage son and two of his friends were discussing Bryce's motorcycle with frank admiration.

"Is there any chance you'd let us try it, Dr. Bryce?" Fernando Lopez wheedled. "We'll be careful, I promise. Just around town a few times."

"Not today, Nando," Bryce said. "But tell you what, tomorrow there might be time for me to take you on a ride around town for a bit."

Fernando scowled, and Cassie had a feeling that the boy had been entertaining images of himself impressing girls while driving the motorcycle all by himself. "It takes a while to learn to ride a motorcycle," she said, hoping to help Fernando understand that he most likely would not have been able to race off down the road even if Bryce had said yes. "But sitting on one while someone else drives can help you learn."

"Enough!" Mrs. Lopez scolded the boys. "Stop bothering the doctors this instant." To Bryce, she said, "You can leave your bike here. No harm will come to it. I'll keep a close eye on it and put these boys to work. They've got better things to do than ogle a motorcycle." She was still shooing the boys away from it as Cassie and Bryce ambled toward town.

The Feria Gastronomica was everything Bryce had promised. The town center was bustling with people milling about food stalls and eating at colorful tables and chairs. Bryce couldn't seem to resist plying her with food, and she couldn't seem to resist eating of it.

"Start with this," he said, handing her an *elote loco*—corn on the cob on a stick, covered with cheese and a tangy sauce. "That way you can still walk around while you're eating and decide what you want to snack on next."

There truly did seem to be every sort of food under the sun available. The smell of grilled meat was irresistible, and she and Bryce munched on shrimp sticks while they chose their next course. They finally sat down at one of the brightly colored tables with a huge plate of beef and chicken alongside rice, salad and tortillas.

Cassie loaded meat and vegetables onto a tortilla and pinched it into a taco. She took a bite and sighed. "Okay, you were right. It was worth rushing to get here so we could do this. This is some of the best food I've had since I got here."

"Surely not better than the food at the camp mess hall!"

She winced. "Don't tell anybody back at the camp, but after trying the *pupusas* here, I'm not sure I can face the ones back at the mess hall. Does saying that make me a terrible person? Our cooks work so hard for us."

"Don't worry," he said. "It'll never get back to camp. I won't tell a soul."

She smiled and gazed into his eyes. "I knew I could trust you." They held each other's gaze for a moment. Cassie had forgotten how warm his eyes could be.

She cleared her throat. "Now what about this waterfall?" she said.

The waterfall was only a short hike from town. The path was visible, but only just; thick overgrown foliage threatened to eliminate it.

"It's a good thing we're here in the late afternoon," said Bryce. "Enough tourists have come through here today that the path is fairly clear. If we'd come earlier, I probably would have had to borrow a machete from Mrs. Lopez to clear our way."

A machete. She pictured Bryce swinging a machete to clear away the tall grass. There was still a lot about El Salvador that she was getting used to.

Pushing the jungle foliage back from the path was hot exhausting work. Bryce traveled in front of Cassie so that he could bear the brunt of the labor. Within moments, both of their shirts were soaked with sweat. Cassie couldn't help but notice the way the muscles tightened under Bryce's white T-shirt as he pushed back the grass and ferns. Then, as if her resolve hadn't been challenged enough for one day, Bryce removed his T-shirt and tied it around his forehead to keep the sweat out of his eyes.

Lord have mercy, Cassie thought. Bryce was perfectly tanned underneath his shirt. Beads of sweat formed along his chest and back, and his jeans hung low on his hips.

The image of a half-naked Bryce leading her through the jungle was going to be with her for a long time. "How far away is it now?" she asked, wondering just how long she was going to be tortured.

"About ten minutes," he replied.

You can handle anything for just ten minutes, she thought.

Finally, they arrived, hot and exhausted.

"Here it is," said Bryce. "Los Chorros de la Calera."

The waterfall consisted of several crystal streams; some strong and thundering, others quiet and fast. Each stream cascaded down a rock face covered with moss and vines, and they all fed into the same pool at the bottom. The sun dappled the surface of the water, and all around her was the fresh smell of the forest: wood and vegetation. It reminded her of the visits she'd made to greenhouses and conservatories in New York, but there, she'd always been aware of the traffic and the throngs of people just outside. Now, she was completely surrounded by greenery, and the mist rising from the waterfall was the only source of coolness in the heat.

"It's beautiful," she breathed, and for a moment she and Bryce simply stood together in the silence. Then she turned toward him, and there it was again—that feeling of old emotions being stirred.

It's just nostalgia, she thought. But as the sounds of the waterfall rushed in her ears, she knew her feelings were about more than just the past. They were about this moment with Bryce, too.

She turned toward him, looking into the warmth of his brown eyes.

And then, in spite of herself, she started to giggle.

"What's amusing you now?" he murmured.

"It's just that it's so beautiful here...with

the light reflecting off the pool and the forest surrounding us…"

"And natural beauty is…funny, somehow?"

"No, natural beauty is breathtaking. What's funny is that amid all of it, you've got a T-shirt tied around your head. With the jungle backdrop, you look like a kid playing Rambo."

"Oh, so you're laughing at *me*. Why don't you take a picture of my amusing headgear so you can show everyone back at the camp?"

"I would, but I left my phone back at Mrs. Lopez's."

"Excellent. Then you won't mind if I do this." He pushed her straight into the pool beneath the falls.

"Bryce!" she shrieked, laughing as her head broke the surface. "That was *completely* uncalled for!" Also shocking and completely unexpected. She'd never been pushed into a body of water in her life. Overprotected and sheltered as she was, no child or adult would ever have dared to do something as unsafe as shove her into a pool. She hadn't even been allowed to swim until she went to college. She remembered going to pool parties on rare occasions as a child, watching sadly from a patio as other children splashed and screamed, pushing each other into the water with reckless abandon.

And now Bryce had just shoved her in. As though she weren't breakable. As though she were just an ordinary person.

"I disagree," he called from the shore. "You looked hot. I helped you cool down. You're welcome."

"We just ate!" she said, with mock annoyance. "What if I got a cramp?"

"Then I guess I'd have to come in after you." And with that, he dove into the pool himself.

He broke the surface beside her. They held on to each other for a moment, gasping for air as they found one another in the water. Her head spun, and she wasn't sure whether it was with excitement or confusion. Maybe it was a mix of both. He'd become so much more carefree, and she loved it.

Without realizing it, she tilted her face toward his and then suddenly, they were kissing.

It was everything she remembered; it was *better* than she remembered. It was even better than the moment under the balsa tree, because this time his arms were wrapped around her and she could feel the full length of his body against hers. And this time, there was no mistaking the kiss for an accident. They hadn't just gotten caught up in the moment. He was kissing her as though he meant to kiss her. She knew it, and she was letting him know in every way she could that she meant to kiss him right back. His lips were heat and salt against hers; his arms wrapped about her and pulled her close with a firmness that felt more right than anything she'd experienced in years.

And then they heard voices coming from the path ahead. They pulled apart just as a group of tourists emerged from the foliage.

Cassie's breath was fast and ragged. She fought for control as she tried to compose herself. "Well. That was certainly something," she said, trying and failing to keep the emotion out of her voice.

"Here, let me help you out of the water."

Was his voice quavering, too? His breath seemed uneven, but that might just be the exertion of swimming to the side of the pool and helping her climb up onto the grass. "We should get back to Mrs. Lopez's," he said. "She's probably getting worried about us."

He was still holding her hand, even though she was already back on dry land. She gave no indication that he needed to let go.

Their eyes met. She had absolutely no idea what to say.

Fortunately, he did.

"I know we've been talking a lot about moving forward," he said. "And if you don't want that to happen again, I completely understand. I won't put you in that position ever again. But I had to take the chance. I needed to make damn sure I left that waterfall without any regrets."

She stepped close to him. "I'm glad," she said.

"That I kissed you?"

"That you took the risk."

Bryce's lips burned as they hacked their way through the foliage back to Mrs. Lopez's house.

He'd known the moment he was going to kiss her again. It had been the moment she'd emerged from the water, laughing. He'd pushed her in completely on impulse, unable to resist her playfulness. And when he'd seen her head break the water, eyes sparkling and face filled with excitement, he'd known that nothing was going to stop him from kissing her again.

And she'd wanted the kiss every bit as much as he did.

But they still had to work together. How would things go once they got back to camp, resumed their daily lives? A kiss by a waterfall made for a pleasant moment, but ultimately, he and Cassie might not be looking for the same things. He'd been down that road with her before, and he didn't want to make the same mistake again. He wanted someone who was serious.

The trouble was, he also wanted someone who kissed him the way Cassie had kissed him just a moment ago. Completely, wholeheartedly, without holding back.

No, he didn't want *someone* who kissed him that way. He wanted it to be Cassie.

He'd meant what he had said. He didn't regret that kiss, not for an instant. But where did it leave the two of them now?

I'm glad that you took the risk, she'd said. But that didn't tell him anything about how she wanted to proceed.

And no matter how they did proceed, there was no way that things could return to the way they had been going at the medical outpost.

Any semblance they'd had of maintaining a professional relationship was slipping away, and fast. He didn't think he could return to being just colleagues with her. And he didn't think that she wanted to take a step back, either.

Her words reverberated in his head again. *I'm glad that you took the risk.* So was he. But the kiss had been a single moment, outside of their normal lives at the camp. Once they returned to their usual daily routines and went back to the daily routine of being colleagues, would she still be interested in a relationship? The familiar worry that she only wanted a fling cropped up.

A kiss was one thing. But neither of them had really talked about what they wanted.

What Bryce wanted was time. Time to see things unfold, see how they felt about one another. Without putting any pressure on either of them, or on the relationship.

But they had to return to camp soon. He wished there were some way that they could delay returning, to give themselves more time to see what happened between the two of them, without forcing anything. And to have the chance to find out what she wanted. How she felt. If she wanted a fling, or if she wanted him.

Or maybe it would be best to simply return to the camp as soon as possible. Maybe they should just see about going back tonight. They were tired, but the moon would be full and bright. He didn't want to get back to the camp anytime soon, but at least, once they did, he'd have a better idea of where they stood.

But when they returned to Mrs. Lopez's, they learned that it would be impossible to return that night.

Tragedy had struck. They were met by a scowling Mrs. Lopez, three shamefaced teenage boys and a heap of mangled metal that was barely recognizable as a motorcycle.

Apparently, all three boys had been riding the bike at once and had lost control while heading toward a ravine. No one had been hurt, but the motorcycle was unsalvageable. The boys had collected the rubble from the ravine and placed it on a blanket in the front lawn. Bryce sifted through the mess of pulverized motorcycle parts, trying to find some way to wrap his mind around what had happened.

Cassie put a hand on his shoulder. "It's okay to be upset."

"I'm not upset."

"No—maybe devastated would be a more apt description. Come on, Bryce. It's obvious how you feel. That bike was your pride and joy."

"It's just a little dented," he said through gritted teeth.

"In twenty places. And the front wheel's bent. And it's been smashed into multiple pieces." She nudged the debris with her foot. "I guess you could salvage the engine and try to build a new motorcycle around it, but at that point…wouldn't it be less expensive to just buy a new bike?"

He felt his stomach roil at her suggestion, even though he knew that what she said was logical. The bike was beyond repair. But he couldn't fathom leaving it behind. Over the past few years, the bike had become a part of him. It had been with him on every mission outside the camp. Riding the bike around the countryside had been his main source of freedom and joy outside of work. He felt as though he were leaving a fellow fallen soldier behind in the field.

"I can't leave it," he said. "You can take a bus back to camp if you like, but I'm staying with the bike." He knew he sounded absurd, but he didn't care.

She knelt beside him. "I know it was more than just a bike to you. I know what it represents. You bought it with the money from the engagement ring you sold. I'm sure that whomever that ring was for, she was someone special. But if she was someone who couldn't see everything you are, all that you have to offer, then she didn't deserve you. And now that it's over, you've got to let it go…just like you've got to let your motorcycle go."

The words came out before he could stop them. "I bought the engagement ring for you." He hadn't ever meant to say it. The words just slipped out. And there was no unsaying them now. He held his breath, waiting for her reaction.

Her eyes widened. Her mouth was set, her jaw determined. He'd seen that look on her face before. It showed up when someone tried to tell her that a patient couldn't be saved or that her treatment plan wouldn't work.

"We've got to save this bike," she said. "We've got to get it to a shop right now."

He shook his head. "No. Cassie, you were right the first time. The bike is done for. The only thing I can do is let it go."

"No, *you* were right. Like you said, it's just got a few dents here and there. Come on, if we gather the corners of the blanket together, I think we can get all the pieces to a shop." She began gathering broken motorcycle parts into her arms.

"Cassie." He took her hands to stop her from picking up more pieces. Her hands were so delicate and soft. She'd have made a great surgeon, if she'd wanted to be one. "There's no saving this bike. It's been with me for years, and now it's time to say goodbye. If there's one thing I've learned, it's that we can't keep living in the past. Let's just focus on what comes next."

With much reluctance, she dropped the armful of parts she'd been holding.

Of all the reactions she could have had to learning that the engagement ring he'd bought had been for her, this was one he'd never imagined. And yet it felt right, somehow. As sad as he was to lose the bike, Cassie's strong reaction had a calming effect on him. She seemed almost as devastated as he was. He wondered if she might be able to understand just how much the bike meant to him.

"I'll arrange for a scrap truck to pick it up tomorrow," he said to Mrs. Lopez.

"I'm so sorry," she said again. "I can't believe those boys would disobey me. I told them they'll be grounded for the rest of their lives."

"I shouldn't have left the keys here," Bryce said. "I should have realized it would be too tempting. The important thing is that no one was hurt."

"How will we get back to camp?" Cassie asked.

"Let's head to the hotel and start fresh in the morning," said Bryce. "We'll probably have to take a chicken bus to get back."

"That doesn't sound quite as glamorous as the way we got here," said Cassie.

He managed a small chuckle. "No, a chicken bus is exactly what it sounds like." They began to walk toward the hotel when Bryce thought of something. "Wait!"

He ran back toward the heap of rubble on the blanket and began sifting through it.

"What are you looking for?" asked Cassie.

"This." He picked up the bike's ignition switch and removed the ring that held the copper casing together. "I want to keep something to remember it by." He pocketed the ignition switch ring and stood up. "I'm ready. Let's get to our hotel."

After the harsh conditions of the medical camp, the luxury of the hotel was a little overwhelming for Cassie. They were staying at a cozy bed-and-breakfast in Juayua, away from the bustle of the central streets. The building was secluded among a grove of palm trees, with a perfectly manicured lawn that was striking after so much untamed jungle foliage. Rocking chairs beckoned invitingly from the front porch, and water bubbled merrily from concrete fountains with statues covered in soft moss.

Cassie was still trying to absorb what she'd learned at the scene of the motorcycle crash. *That engagement ring was for me. He bought the ring for me, which means he was going to propose. And then I broke up with him.*

Everything about the past five years could have been different. She'd never known he'd bought a ring. Never even known he'd been thinking about marriage. If he'd asked her, back then, would she have said yes? She couldn't say, but she saw how a future with him could have been possible. And she saw, for the first time, just how much she'd given up. She'd known, at the time, that she was giving up the most important relationship she'd ever had. But she hadn't really thought about the future she was giving up, as well.

An alternative life flashed through her mind. She and Bryce could have been married by now. Maybe even started a family together. She pushed away thoughts of sandy-haired children with Bryce's warm brown eyes.

It wasn't meant to be, she thought. She and Bryce had both had things they needed to

learn. Bryce had had to find himself, away
from his family's high expectations, just as
she'd needed to learn who she was, away from
her family's overprotectiveness.

Another thought occurred to her. *He
bought the bike with money from the ring
that he got for me. So it's like I've been with
him all this time.*

Bryce had looked so sad as he stared at the
wreckage of the bike. Was it because of the
motorcycle itself or because of what it represented?

She only knew that the second she'd heard
the ring was meant for her, she'd wanted to
save the bike at all costs. But Bryce was right.
It was completely pulverized. There was no
saving it now.

If the bike represented their relationship,
and now it was completely destroyed, what
did that mean for the two of them? She could
probably make herself crazy by trying to read
something into that.

She would have done anything to fix the
motorcycle, if there had only been hope. But
it was too badly damaged. She wondered if
it was the same for her and Bryce. Yesterday,
she had worried that there'd been so much
damage that the two of them could never be
anything more than friends. But today, there

had been that kiss at the waterfall. She could still hear the roar of the waterfall in her ears, the heat and the feeling of Bryce so close to her again. She could still feel exactly how her body had responded.

The concierge seemed to be taking an awfully long time getting them checked in.

Cassie marveled at the beauty of the hotel lobby. How did she and Bryce keep finding themselves in such romantic settings? The road full of wildflowers, the waterfall and now this secluded hotel.

Just watch. The way this day has been going, they'll probably tell us that there's only one room available, and then I'll have to deal with sleeping in the same room as Bryce on top of everything else.

Finally, the concierge placed a set of keys on the counter. "I'm afraid there are only two rooms available, and they're quite a way down the hall from one another," he said.

"That's perfect," Cassie replied, laughing inwardly with relief. It seemed that at least for tonight, she and Bryce would not be sleeping tantalizingly close to one another.

"In fact, they're on separate floors," the concierge continued. "If you'd like, I could try to see if we can ask a guest to move…"

"Separate floors is fine," Bryce said hastily, grabbing the keys and giving one to Cassie. "Looks like you're on one, and I'm on three." They gave one another an awkward wave goodbye, and Cassie watched as Bryce headed toward the third floor.

Her room was bright and cozy. She showered, reveling in the seemingly limitless supply of hot water.

It was almost impossible to get her mind off the ring. *Why didn't he tell me?* she thought again, wrapping herself in one towel and using another on her hair.

Had he thought she would say no? Had he been afraid to take the risk? She wasn't sure there was any way she'd ever be able to know for sure.

She heard a knock on the door.

She tucked the towel around her body a little tighter, and gave her hair one last tumble with the other towel before tossing it aside. She looked through the peephole in the door and saw that it was Bryce.

What did he want with her?

From the way he'd responded to her during that kiss, she had a feeling she knew. She wasn't certain, but she thought—she hoped—that Bryce was about to take another risk. And if he was, then this time she was determined not to pass up her chance to show him exactly how she felt.

She let the door swing open, and Bryce walked in. A second later, she was in his arms. The towel barely made a sound as it fell to the floor.

CHAPTER EIGHT

HE PRESSED HER into his arms, slamming the door shut behind him with his foot as he pulled her body into his. As her towel fell from her body, she felt the roughness of his clothes against her naked skin. An electric heat crackled between them as he bent to kiss her again.

For weeks, her mind had swirled with *what-ifs*. What if Bryce thought she was just out for a thrill? What if that first kiss had only been about nostalgia? What if they were only getting caught up in the moment, influenced by their romantic settings?

But there was nothing uncertain about what was happening now. He kissed her in a way that claimed her. He held her body close as he entered the hotel room and leaned her against the wall, his tongue exploring every corner of her mouth.

And she kissed him back just as ardently,

hoping to make her intentions clear. For days, she'd been looking for a chance to show him exactly how she felt. Now that chance was here, and she wasn't going to waste it.

Bryce's kisses began to move down to her jawline. He made his way down her neck, and the crook of her shoulder, and then lower, to the first rise of her breast. She leaned her head back and moaned in response to the heat of his mouth against her skin.

A yearning had been stirring in her body for weeks. That yearning was fully awake now, and for the first time, she didn't feel she had to hold it back.

And then his mouth was on hers again, and as his hands found her breasts she couldn't think anymore. She was lost in sensation. The traces of cedar and spice that had teased her since her arrival covered her body now. The fabric of his shirt, rough against her bare skin, both chafed and tantalized. Her fingers trembled as she reached to undo the buttons. She slid the shirt from his back, *finally* able to touch his naked chest after weeks of burning to feel his skin against hers. The room was quiet except for the rustle of their bodies moving together, but the roar of her pulse in her ears drowned out everything except the small voice inside her that screamed, *Don't stop!*

She wholeheartedly agreed with that voice. She didn't want to stop. Except for one thing.

She wrenched herself away from Bryce's kiss. "There's something I need to tell you," she said.

"What?" His breathing was heavy, ragged.

"It's been…a long time, since I've done this."

"How long?"

Five years, four months and twenty-two days. She hesitated. She didn't want to tell him. It was embarrassing. And yet…

Show him how you feel, the voice inside her urged. If she was going to get her chance, this was it.

His eyes bored into hers. "How long, Cassie?"

"About five years."

Something in his face changed. If he'd been eager before, now he almost looked hungry. As though her words, far from slowing him down, had sparked renewed desire. He kissed her with renewed urgency, and her mouth opened to his as she desperately tried to give him all the unspoken words and pent-up emotions that she hadn't known how to express.

They were still leaning against the wall. He held her body against his, hands pressed against the small of her back as they advanced farther into the room. He walked her back until her thighs touched the edge of the four-poster bed, and then he toppled her onto it with a gentle push. He kicked off his shoes, then pulled a small packet from his pocket. Ah. Protection. She was glad to see that this was at least one way in which Bryce hadn't changed. He was still looking out for them both.

He shoved his jeans off and stood before her in his boxers. She took in everything she'd wanted to see since her first day here. Well, almost everything. His body was familiar, but different in all the ways she'd anticipated it to be. His thighs were smooth and muscled, his torso defined. His tan covered his whole body.

And if there had been any doubt up to this point about the way he felt about her, it fell away as she saw the full evidence of his attraction beneath his boxers. He eased those off now, and let her look her fill. He stood before her, vulnerable, exposed...and wanting her.

"I missed this view," she said.

"You're not the only one," he replied. He stepped forward, slipping onto the bed with her, his body alongside hers.

"There were some other things I missed, too."

"Oh? Like this?" He leaned forward and kissed her.

"Yes."

"And this?" He stroked her breast and planted a slow kiss on one nipple.

"Yes."

"How about this?" He slipped his hand away from her breast, down the length of her body and to the top of her thigh. Her legs fell apart as she felt his hand between them, searching for the sensitive little nub between her legs. His thumb glided back and forth with slow, smooth strokes, and she began to melt with pleasure.

He lifted his body atop hers, and she could feel him hard and ready at her entrance. "Now," she whispered, and he eased himself into her, in one long slow thrust. He gathered her hair into his fingers and pressed her lips toward his, and on instinct she wrapped her legs around his waist, pulling him in even deeper.

Their hips rocked together in a dance that was timeless, familiar and yet somehow entirely new. As his strokes increased in their intensity, she felt her body responding to his, a heat rising within her core. Her mouth yielded to his, over and over, and her body hovered on the brink of ecstasy. Finally, unable to resist the sensation of her body moving with his, she let herself go, her mind spinning past a place where thought existed. He continued thrusting into her for a moment longer and then shuddered before he sank beside her onto the bed.

Her body was nerveless, replete with satisfaction. She could barely move, but as his lips sought hers once more, she lifted her head to his before resting it against his chest.

They lay with their arms and legs tangled together. She neither knew nor cared where he ended and she began. She felt him tracing one of her shoulders lightly with his finger, and despite her best efforts, the soothing caress began to lull her into sleep.

As she drifted off, she felt Bryce pull her closer against his chest. Her last thought before she fell asleep was that she'd never have had the courage to show up at Bryce's hotel room.

But she was so glad he'd taken the risk of coming to hers.

Bryce woke first early the next morning. He'd always been an early riser. It was a good quality for a surgeon. In his residency days, he'd sometimes had to wake at 5:00 a.m. or even earlier to begin his day. He'd never been able to break the habit of waking up just before dawn, even now, when his surgical career was long over. Now, with the exception of the occasional emergency, he could usually count on sleeping through the night and enjoying a leisurely morning.

He hoped that he and Cassie would be able to spend this leisurely morning together. There was no hurry to get back to the camp, and after last night, they needed some time to get their bearings with one another. Everything had happened so fast.

After their kiss at the waterfall, Bryce had known that he wasn't going to be able to set his growing attraction for Cassie aside. But he hadn't expected himself to act on it, at least not so quickly. But then he'd seen her reaction after he'd told her about the engagement ring. She had looked at the crashed motorcycle and understood exactly how he felt about it.

He hadn't wanted to admit it, but for five years, he'd carried Cassie with him in one way or another. First by holding on to the engagement ring, then by pawning the ring and using the money for his motorcycle. And also by holding on to the anger and resentment he'd felt for so long. It had been all he had left of her, and he had been unwilling to let it go. Until she came back into his life, and he realized just how simple it could be to let it go.

He'd wrestled with his thoughts in his own hotel room for less than ten minutes before running down to Cassie's. He didn't know for sure if she wanted any more than the kiss they'd shared. But nothing could stop him from finding out.

In the heat of the moment, he hadn't cared that he was once again putting himself in a vulnerable position with her. It was one thing to act on physical feelings. It was quite another to take the risk of telling her how he felt. Or of asking how she felt. She'd certainly responded enthusiastically…but sex, he supposed, could mean anything. It didn't mean she wanted a relationship.

Had it really been five years since Cassie had had sex? That he was the last person she'd been intimate with. Although he hadn't thought about it much, he'd assumed that Cassie had probably had other partners over the years. But apparently not.

Ever since Cassie had come to El Salvador, it seemed that so many of his assumptions about her were untrue. He'd always thought of her as a bit reckless, a bit of a daredevil, but he knew now that was only one side of her.

Unlike him, Cassie was not an early riser and never had been. He watched her sleep, the sun peeking in through the blinds and casting shadows on her face. He ran his hands through her short hair, gently, careful not to wake her. He still wanted her. He'd been trying so hard to push his feelings away because he wasn't sure what she wanted. But last night, his desire had taken over.

But giving in to one night of desire didn't change the fact that he and Cassie might want very different things. No matter how he felt about Cassie, he still wanted a committed relationship. He'd had his share of flings, as well as his share of heartbreak. The next time he got emotionally involved with someone, he wanted it to be with someone interested in the long term, who might even want to start a family someday. He had no idea if that was what Cassie wanted. From everything they'd discussed about what had brought her to El Salvador, he had the distinct impression that she'd come here to escape predictability and routine. She may not be the same reckless daredevil he remembered, but he knew that she liked thrills and excitement just as much as ever. She'd told him about how much she needed to get out of the routine of her daily life in New York. What if her night with him was about nothing more than reconnecting with that adventurous side of herself?

He did not regret their night together for an instant. But he also didn't want to set himself up for more pain. He'd misunderstood Cassie's feelings for him in the past, and so he'd need to guard his heart now. Which meant telling her, as soon as possible, that he was looking for more in a relationship than she might be willing to pursue at this point in her life.

They'd have to have The Talk about how they were going to figure out continuing to work together. The sooner they had The Talk, the better.

He'd been trying to keep quiet next to her, but suddenly both of their phones began to vibrate. Hers was across the room, inside her open travel bag, while his was next to the nightstand. Cassie opened bleary eyes at the noise. "Whuzzit?" she mumbled.

Bryce grabbed his phone from beside the bed. "It's a text from the camp," he said.

Cassie sat up, wide-awake. "What's it say?"

"There's an emergency. They need all doctors who are off base to return to the camp as soon as possible. There've been more rockfalls up in the mountains. They need all hands on deck to cope with the influx of injuries coming in. We've got to get back as soon as we can."

They looked at one another in dismay.

"I was hoping we'd have time this morning to talk about…things," said Cassie.

"Me, too. We'll have to save our conversation for the bus. Speaking of which, we should start making arrangements to get back right away." He got out of the bed and stretched. "I'll take our stuff down to the lobby and figure out our transportation home. You can meet me there when you're ready."

She nodded. He wanted to lean in for a kiss, but wasn't sure if it was a good idea. After all, they hadn't had The Talk yet. In the end, he gave her an awkward kiss on the forehead and rushed out the door.

Cassie brushed her teeth with haste. She knew the bus trip back to camp would take several hours, but that was all the more reason to leave as soon as they could. Unfortunately, it meant that there might not be much time to talk with Bryce about what had happened.

Sex is what happened. You had sex for the first time in five years, four months—oh, who cares. The point is, it's time to reset the counter.

Indeed it was.

She'd felt vulnerable telling Bryce about her five-year dry spell, but she'd wanted him to know. Especially after he'd told her about the engagement ring. He'd kept that a secret from her for such a long time, clearly nervous about how she might respond. But telling her about the ring had changed everything. Until that moment, she'd been determined to show Bryce how she'd felt about him. But, of course, the way he felt about her was just as important.

She hoped that Bryce understood how she felt. She wasn't sure what to make of his brief kiss—on the forehead, of all places—as he'd left to make their travel arrangements. He'd been so brusque. Not unkind, but not exactly melting with emotion, either.

She wondered if he were worried about how they were going to handle working together and being in a relationship at the same time. In a way, it had been simpler five years ago, when their relationship had been a secret. They didn't have to sort out any workplace complications, because they'd simply tried their best to pretend they weren't dating while they were at work. Now, they'd probably have some complexities to work out, and she could imagine that Bryce was as worried as she was about potential pitfalls and how to avoid them.

Or so she assumed. They hadn't had time to discuss much of anything. Certainly not something as complicated as their relationship status. They hadn't even had time to talk about whether they were in a relationship at all.

She headed to the lobby, where Bryce had arranged their passage on a bus that would take them back to Miraflores. When she found him, he was talking with Enrique over the phone about the emergency. Enrique was planning to come back from San Salvador to help out with the victims of the rockfall. He would pick them up in Miraflores, and they'd all head back to camp together. Cassie felt a preemptive twinge of awkwardness as she thought about adding another person to their party so soon after her intimate night with Bryce. She wished they could have more time away from the camp so that she and Bryce could have some space to figure out what they were to each other, as well as what they wanted to tell other people. But as things were, it looked as though they would have to do most of their talking on the bus. If they were even going to talk at all.

The chicken buses of El Salvador weren't

exactly modern, but they were convenient. Although Cassie would have preferred to travel by motorcycle, she'd been interested in trying out the chicken buses since she'd arrived. She'd noticed them everywhere on the road to Juayua; their bright colors were hard to miss. The name "chicken bus" referred to the occasional practice of passengers bringing on chickens or other livestock. As she boarded the bus that morning, there wasn't a chicken in sight, although she did hear faint clucking noises from the back of the bus.

"I know it's probably different from what you're used to, but it's one of the most practical ways to get around," Bryce said.

"It's perfect," said Cassie. "And it sounds like it's the fastest option we have for getting back to the camp to help out."

"The driver says the trip will take about two hours," said Bryce. "We're lucky to get on early in the morning. The buses can get pretty crowded later in the day, but we should miss the worst of it."

"Two hours," said Cassie. "It sounds like we'll have some time to talk, you and I."

He settled down beside her as the bus took off with a lurch. "I suppose it does. Look, last night…" He faltered.

She felt her stomach plummet. What was it

that was so hard for him to say? Did he think last night was a mistake? Her head spun at the thought. She'd been determined not to let go of him again, but if Bryce didn't feel the same way she did, she might not have any choice in the matter.

"What is it?" she said. "Don't you think we should talk about it? Especially given that we work together? We need to figure out what we're going to tell everyone else."

"But we need to figure out what we're telling ourselves first."

It was the way she felt, too, but somehow, the way he said it filled her with trepidation.

"Look," he continued, "last night was fun. But I'll understand if you don't want anything like that to happen again."

She stared at him, aghast.

"Why do you keep saying things like that?" she said. "First after the waterfall in Juayua and now, after this? Why would you assume I wouldn't want this to happen again?"

"Because I don't know what you want," he said.

She couldn't believe it. "I thought I made it pretty clear last night that I wanted you."

"You did. For last night. But I'm not sure what that means for the future."

Hadn't she made it clear, last night, that he

meant something to her? That sleeping with him meant something, just as their relationship had meant something?

Apparently not.

They both stared at each other. She realized that they were at a stalemate. One of them was going to have to take a risk and share their feelings. She was just about to speak when he did.

"Didn't you have fun, as well?" he said.

Fun? Well, she supposed she'd had fun, too. It just wasn't the first word she would have chosen to describe their evening.

Words like *intimate* or *special* or *earth-shattering* would be her preferred adjectives.

"I didn't *not* have fun," she said.

He instantly looked hurt.

"What I mean is that it was more than fun for me," she continued quickly. "This was something that I've been hoping would happen from the moment I arrived in El Salvador."

"Me, too," he said, his voice tinged with emotion.

Relief flooded through her. "It's just been so long since I've had any real excitement in my life. For the past few years, it's all been about work and about making sure other people have what they need. People who have everything they need, but who can still manage to be pretty demanding. But yesterday, I finally felt like myself again, after trying to be someone else for so long. It was like the adventurous person I used to be was still there, just waiting for me to let her out. And you helped me do that, Bryce."

He looked as though she had slapped him. "I see," he said. "So, just to be clear, last night was all about you kind of getting back in touch with your old self?"

How had she managed to say the wrong thing? She tried to reassure him.

"I just meant that I couldn't have done that without you. I was trying to explain what last night meant to me. And I'd really like to know what it meant to you."

He was silent for a long moment, and then he said, "This is what I was afraid of. All this time, you've been trying to get back to your old self. But I remember who you were, too. You're someone who's always in search of excitement, and being here gives you a chance to find it. Being *with me* gives you a chance to find it."

Cassie was horrified. Did Bryce still think that for her, last night was just about finding a thrill? Even after everything they'd been through in the last twenty-four hours, all the ways in which she had tried to express how much he meant to her, she couldn't believe that that was still how he thought about her.

"Bryce, after last night, didn't it feel to you as though something had changed between us? Didn't it feel *at all* as though something new was happening?"

He was quiet for a long time. Then his brown eyes pierced her heart as he said, "I thought that last night was about us. But it seems like it was about you. I'm glad you found yourself, I really am. But I'm looking for something more."

"Wait. Just let me explain. My words didn't come out right the first time. Will you please just listen?"

He leaned back in his seat. "I'm not going anywhere for a while."

"Ever since I was born, my diagnosis ruled my life. People were constantly telling me what I couldn't do. And so once my heart was healthy, I was determined to do everything that I couldn't do before. And I know that right at the height of my rebellious phase, I met you. You got caught up in my determination to prove myself. And that wasn't fair to you, because it probably felt like I put our relationship second to maybe…wanting an adventure or a thrill. But I don't know if anyone's ever really been able to understand what that means to me. For me, being adventurous is about living life to the last drop. It's about affirming that I actually am alive. Because I couldn't really live for the first years of my life. I was just surviving."

He nodded thoughtfully. "So last night was one of those life-affirming experiences?"

"Yes. But it was also special, because it was with you."

He seemed more relaxed now, and she took that as a good sign. "Maybe we shouldn't put too much pressure or expectations on ourselves, and just see where things go," she said.

"Fair enough," he replied. "But what do we tell people back at the camp?"

She thought for a moment. "Do we...have to tell them anything? Maybe we could keep things just between ourselves for a while. Get a sense of how we feel before we go telling other people about how we feel."

He nodded, but she wasn't sure how to read his expression. For a while, last night, Bryce had surprised her with his willingness to take chances. But at this moment, he seemed as guarded as ever.

The chicken bus lurched from side to side as it lumbered down the road. Cassie had fallen asleep, and her head dropped against Bryce's shoulder. He didn't mind it there. But their conversation had left him with a sense of unease.

He wasn't sure exactly how they were defining their relationship after their talk. He liked the idea of staying open to see where things would go, but he wasn't certain he wanted to forgo telling their colleagues anything at all. He'd done the secret relationship thing with Cassie before.

She just wants the excitement, a nagging voice said in the back of his mind.

That wasn't fair, though. It made sense not to tell their colleagues at the camp about their relationship while they were waiting to understand it themselves.

And he'd been touched by how Cassie had explained her search for excitement. How she'd spent her childhood feeling not as though she were living but merely surviving. What must it have been like, for a young, ambitious Cassie, to be cooped up in a recovery room for months on end? To be prevented from going out and exploring the world? He could certainly relate to the frustration of a long, slow recovery, constantly being told what he could or could not do. His hands trembled a bit as he recalled the early days of his recovery after the accident. Everyone had told him to take things slow, but he'd been desperate to push his recovery as far as possible, to prove what he could do, instead of wallowing in grief over what he'd lost. Finding the patience to take things slow had been one of the hardest parts of his recovery.

He realized that he had just missed the perfect opportunity to tell Cassie about the accident. Except he couldn't. What had she said? *It's about living life to the last drop.*

What would she think if she knew that coming to El Salvador wasn't about living his life but about hiding from it? Here, he was safe from the sympathetic looks of former friends who knew everything he'd lost. He was safe from anyone who might compare him to the gifted surgeon he used to be and find he didn't measure up. He was safe from family gatherings where everyone was a surgeon except for him, sharing a bond that he no longer had access to.

Cassie had said that he had helped her to find her old self. How would she feel if she knew it was all a sham? That no matter how many risks he took here, no matter how many daring things he did, none of it felt more frightening to him than going back to New York and being faced with the expectations that everyone held there. He gave a short laugh. Cassie had wanted to find her old self, while Bryce wanted nothing more than to get away from the past. From Bryce Hamlin, superstar surgeon, and all of the pressure that went with living up to that reputation.

He was glad to know that for Cassie, last night had been about more than just excitement. And he could understand that to her, being a thrill-seeker meant something more than it did to most. But what about what the two of them meant to each other?

He couldn't forget that he'd misread her before. He reminded himself that he couldn't expect to form a long-term relationship with someone who didn't feel the same way. He needed to guard his heart until he learned what Cassie wanted: an adventure or him? Or perhaps both?

He wondered if Cassie even knew the answer.

CHAPTER NINE

THEY ARRIVED BACK at the camp in the late afternoon, and jumped right into work. They had no time to rest or get their bearings—the camp was in chaos. Bryce left their luggage next to the main office building, surprised that little Manny hadn't run up to greet them or take their things back to their cabins for them.

Medical workers were moving quickly through the camp. Bryce saw Anna, the midwife, racing toward a tent with some bandages, and he asked her how they could help.

"Everything happened so fast," Anna said. "At first there was a huge influx of patients all at once, but then the flow started to slow to a trickle about an hour ago. We think everyone who sustained injuries is here at the camp now. We're trying to triage and take them one at a time. The best thing you could do would be to grab a patient and get moving."

Bryce moved through the camp, assisting with triage so that the worst injured patients would get help first. As he continued to work his way through the wounded, he became increasingly aware of the absence of his ten-year-old shadow. Usually the boy was the first to greet him when he got back to the camp and was constantly underfoot with questions, even during emergencies. He was helpful, too, as he could often be sent to run messages between the camp doctors. His worry began to grow, until he saw something that confirmed his worst fear: Mrs. Martinez standing outside one of the medical tents holding Rosibel, tears streaming down her face.

He gripped her arm in reassurance as he headed into a tent, where Manny lay on a camp cot. A nasty gash was evident on the boy's forehead, but as Bryce examined him, he became increasingly concerned about injuries he couldn't see.

Manny tried to sit up, and Bryce put his hand on the boy's too-thin shoulder to keep him lying down.

"Do you know who I am, Manny?"

The boy seemed to be fighting to stay awake. "They told me to wait here," he responded. "But I can't stay. I have to look after

Rosibel." The baby gave a cry that Mrs. Martinez quickly hushed.

As Bryce continued his examination, he was aware that Cassie had quietly entered the tent. Manny asked for his mother a few more times, but didn't seem to hear when Mrs. Martinez tried to reassure him. After a few more moments, he didn't respond at all as Bryce tried to rouse him.

"Subdural hematoma," murmured Cassie.

"We don't know for sure," he said. "Not without a CT scan."

"And we're not going to get a CT scan out here. A hospital in San Salvador might have one, but there's no time to get him there. The confusion, the loss of consciousness—it all points to subdural hematoma. We need to relieve the pressure on his brain, fast."

He knew she was right. Manny's symptoms indicated that he had suffered a blow to the head, possibly multiple blows. The trauma had resulted in a buildup of blood between the brain and skull. Each passing second put Manny at increased risk as the pressure on the brain from the bleeding increased. They needed to operate as quickly as possible.

"Is my son going to die?" asked Mrs. Martinez.

"We'll do everything we can," said Cassie.

"There's bleeding that is putting pressure on his brain. We need to drill a small hole into his skull, and we might have to put in something called a shunt in order to drain the pressure. I know it sounds scary, but if we don't do it, Manny might never wake up."

Mrs. Martinez looked terrified, but she nodded. "Do whatever you need to do. I trust you, Doctor."

"The good news is that you're in very safe hands," Cassie said. "Bryce used to be one of the best surgeons in New York, before he got into obstetrics and started delivering babies. Manny couldn't ask for a better doctor to do this operation than Bryce."

Dread settled like a block of ice into Bryce's stomach. If they didn't relieve the pressure on Manny's brain quickly, he could die. But to do such a procedure here, without the benefit of modern equipment and a full staff, was daunting. Worst of all, he knew that the greatest need at this moment wasn't for modern equipment or a staff of doctors with impressive credentials.

What they needed most of all was a pair of steady hands.

"Cassie," he murmured, "can I have a word?"

She stepped away from Mrs. Martinez. "What is it?"

"I don't think I can do this."

She put her hand on his arm. "I can understand why you're nervous. It's been a while since you practiced. But there's no one else here who has more experience than you with a procedure like this, even if it's been a few years since you performed one."

"It's not that. I just don't think I can drill into Manny's skull."

"I know you care about him. The camp wouldn't be the same without him. But you can't let your feelings interfere with the operation. I don't like the thought of drilling into the cranium, either. It terrifies me. But at least you've done it before. And even though it's a dangerous procedure...even though he might die if you do it..."

"He'll definitely die if I don't," he finished for her. He knew the line. Her face was a mirror image of what it had been five years ago, when she'd said almost those exact words, and convinced him to perform an operation that had impacted their relationship and his career.

But she'd said them because she was convinced that there was no alternative. And just as he had then, he agreed with her. There was certainly no alternative now. The longer they did nothing, the more likely the subdural hematoma was to increase its pressure on Manny's brain.

"All right," he said. His voice was firm, decisive. "Let's get him prepped with anesthesia."

Maybe his tremor wouldn't flare up, he thought. As long as he kept calm, the chances of it flaring were small. And the procedure would be brief. He'd drill for a few seconds at most, just enough to open a hole in the cranium and relieve the pressure on the brain. As long as he stayed relaxed and focused, everything would be fine. The faster he worked, the less chance there would be of any complications.

For a moment, as the nurses prepped Manny for surgery, Bryce almost felt like his old self again. It was just like the days of his surgical residency. Once again, he was the one expected to step up to handle a dangerous, difficult case. And once again, Cassie was looking at him as though she relied on him. As though she trusted him.

Ultimately, it was her look of trust that stopped him.

Cassie had faith in him. Not to perform surgery, but to do the right thing. And he knew that he couldn't operate on Manny just because he wanted to feel like a surgeon again. The risk of his hands trembling at the wrong moment was simply too great.

He couldn't put someone in danger. Especially not someone he cared about.

He lowered the drill. "I can't do it," he said. He saw the surprise in her eyes above her surgical mask. He knew he needed to explain quickly, in a way that would brook no argument. Every second counted. "I have a hand tremor. I can usually control it, but I can't always predict when it will flare up. I can't do this operation. It's too risky."

He put the drill into Cassie's hands and closed her fingers around it.

To her credit, Cassie didn't hesitate, although she must have been shocked to find herself to be the one holding the drill. But if she did feel shocked, she didn't show it. She simply took Bryce's place at Manny's head.

"Show me exactly where to drill and for how long," she said.

Bryce was relieved that she hadn't stopped him with any further questions. He knew that Cassie would always put her patient's well-being above her curiosity, but he was sure that he would have questions to answer the moment the surgery was over.

He showed Cassie where to place the drill. With luck, they would be able to suction the blood out through the hole.

Cassie's hands were perfectly steady as she drilled the hole, stopping exactly when Bryce gave the word. Bryce was relieved as he saw that blood immediately began to drain from the hole. There would be no need for a shunt—Cassie had performed the procedure beautifully, and they could close as soon as the blood had finished draining.

"You're doing great," he said to Cassie. Her face was white as a sheet.

"Glad to hear it," she breathed. He could almost feel how still she was trying to be as the fluid drained from Manny's head. "I have to say, this is a first. When you deliver babies, you typically don't require the use of a drill."

"Just keep your hands steady. We're almost there."

Finally, enough fluid had drained that they could close the scalp. He showed Cassie where to stitch the scalp, but she was already starting to press the edges of the incision together as he spoke. He straightened his back and went outside to where Mrs. Martinez was waiting.

"Manny came through the procedure just fine," he said as she cried tears of relief. "He should start coming round in a few hours. We'll monitor him for at least seventy-two hours, but the procedure went smoothly. He'll need to keep still for a long time, but he should be feeling better soon."

"Oh, thank you," said Mrs. Martinez. She rushed inside the tent to be near her son.

It was starting to rain. Bryce could feel a few drops at first, and then a stronger, steady patter. He couldn't bring himself to move back inside the tent. He wanted just a moment to breathe, to feel relieved that Manny's procedure had gone well.

But his relief was short-lived. As Mrs. Martinez went into the tent, Cassie came out, her eyes blazing.

"What the hell just happened, Bryce?"

"You saved a child's life."

"Bullshit! You know that's not what I'm talking about. You hesitated. You handed the reins over to me at a crucial moment, just like you did with that complicated C-section. What's going on? Why aren't you doing surgical procedures?"

"I told you why, in there." He held up his hands. The tremor was faint, but it was visible. "Can you see it?"

"My god, Bryce, how long has that been going on?"

"Since a few weeks after we broke up."

He saw the realization dawn on her face.

"I was in a car accident, just after you left. Hit on the expressway by a drunk driver. The physical therapy helped quite a bit afterward, but I was never able to recover the full use of my hands."

"So that was the reason you lost your job. That was why you changed specialties. You couldn't be a surgeon anymore. Not with a hand tremor." She gave a low dark laugh. "And to think that when I first got here, I was worried that it might have had something to do with me."

She was still slowly shaking her head. The expression on her face was incredulous. "I can't imagine what the recovery must have been like."

Her continued silence was making him anxious, and he spoke nervously to fill the gap. "There's still a lot I can do," he said. "For a while, I thought I'd never be able to be a physician again. But then one of my mentors recommended obstetrics. There's a lot I can do that doesn't involve surgery. Most of the procedures that come my way are pretty low risk."

"How could you not tell me this?"

"It was five years ago. Does it really matter anymore?"

"Yes! Yes, it matters! Why didn't you call me, why didn't you say anything? You were in a major life-changing accident. No matter what happened between us, if you'd called me, I would have been there for you."

His jaw tightened. "I didn't want your pity."

"I wouldn't have offered you pity. I would have offered you support. I would have been there for you. I didn't know. I wish you had called me. I wish you hadn't had to go through your recovery alone."

"You left a note that indicated you didn't want any calls from me."

"And that was a mistake. It was a stupid mistake! But I couldn't have known you were going to be in an accident. I didn't know you were going to lose your profession. You loved being a surgeon. It was everything to you. And you were so gifted."

There, he could see it in her eyes. Pity. The exact response that he didn't want from her.

He'd spent the past three years in El Salvador trying to escape from the shadow of Bryce Hamlin, genius surgeon. He'd tried to carve out a life for himself in New York, and it hadn't worked. Everywhere he turned, everyone—whether they were colleagues, family or friends—wanted to talk about the doctor he *used* to be. The person he used to be. No one seemed to be able to talk to him without comparing him to his past, pre-accident self.

But he wasn't that person anymore. Even though everyone seemed to regret that that version of him was gone. Even though Cassie now stood before him, expressing her pity that he was no longer the surgeon he had been.

He realized that she'd done the same thing she'd done when she came into his life five years ago. Back then, she opened his life to more excitement. She pushed him to take more risks. Just as she unwittingly had today. Even though she hadn't known about his hands, she'd still pushed him to do the procedure on Manny. That was who Cassie was. She pushed him, challenged him, made him take risks he hadn't even known were there.

But letting her back into his heart was a risk he couldn't take. Because along with all the memories of how she pushed him, came all the feelings of heartbreak after things had gone too far.

He'd already survived that heartbreak once. He knew he would never be able to survive it again.

"Cassie," he said. "We need to end this."

"What do you mean?"

"I mean us. We need to stop, the two of us. We aren't going to be able to make it work."

Tears mixed with rainwater streamed down her face.

"I don't understand," she said.

"Because I'm not the rock star surgeon anymore. More than that, I'm not the *person* I used to be. But I think you might still need that person in your life. Everything you said today on the bus made me realize that you want an adventure. And I think that's a wonderful thing. It's even something I want, a lot of the time. But it's not something I want from a relationship."

Her lips barely moved, and he had to strain to hear her against the rainfall as she said, "Is that all you think I want from a relationship?"

He didn't know. But he didn't think he could handle the disappointment of finding out.

Not again.

"Let's just call it what it was," he said. "A trip down memory lane. The sooner we stop holding on to the people we used to know, the sooner we can both focus on our futures."

Her chin trembled, and he could hear her trying to keep her voice steady. "I'm not holding on to anyone I used to know. Because I don't think I ever really knew you. I sure as hell don't know you now."

She turned and left, leaving him standing there in the rain.

Strange, he thought, as she walked away. Right after the breakup, he had fantasized about what it would feel like if he had been the one to initiate the breakup. He'd nursed his hurt and his anger, and he'd thought he wanted a chance to show her how it felt, to hurt her the way she'd hurt him. But as he watched her walk into the darkness, he knew that turning the tables wasn't satisfying at all.

Cassie bunched her pillow into a ball. She'd tried a hundred different pillow positions and multiple corners of her mattress, but she couldn't get comfortable enough to sleep. The rain pounded on the roof of her quarters. She was exhausted from a long day of travel and treating patients injured by the mountain rockfall. But sleep would not come. She'd been tossing and turning for hours with little success. She checked the time on the cell phone next to her bed. Three in the morning. If she was going to get any rest before her shift started in four hours, she needed to drift off soon.

The trouble was, it was hard to sleep when you were heartbroken and furious with someone at the same time.

She turned onto her other side, trying to block out the noise of the rain with her extra pillow. Stupid raindrops. There was no way she was ever going to fall asleep with it pounding on the roof, insistent as a drum.

Oh, who are you kidding? she thought. Her sleeplessness had nothing to do with the rain, and everything to do with Bryce and what he'd said earlier that evening.

She had thought he'd be willing to give their relationship a chance. Instead, he'd cut things off abruptly. Before they'd even gotten off the ground. What was he thinking?

Just twenty-four hours before, they'd made love. And now, she wasn't sure he ever wanted to look at her again.

What did you expect? she asked herself. *He put his heart on the line for you once, and got it broken. You should have known he wouldn't be able to do it now.*

He'd told her that he thought she wanted an adventure. It confirmed everything she had feared. Despite her best efforts, despite everything she'd tried to show him, she had failed. She had hurt him too badly five years ago. He was never going to believe that he'd been more to her than an exciting thrill.

And now things were over between them, almost before they'd begun.

She wondered, for the millionth time, why he hadn't called and told her about the accident. No matter what had happened between them, he should have known that she would have been there to support him through something like that.

But maybe he hadn't wanted her support at that particular time. And if he thought that he'd been nothing more than a fling to her, then it made sense that he wouldn't call.

At the very least, he could have told her about his hand tremor when she arrived at the camp. But he'd kept that a secret, as well. She thought about how Bryce had claimed that it had been freeing to give up surgery. To her, it didn't sound as though he felt it had been freeing. It sounded as though the pain of the breakup had been compounded by the pain of the accident.

When he'd told her that she would be the one to drill into Manny's skull, she'd almost wondered if he'd lost his mind. She couldn't believe that he would turn such an important procedure over to her. And she trusted him. She'd been so confident that he would be able to help. The situation was dire, but she'd known that Bryce, of all people, was the perfect person to handle it. His natural caution and his surgical expertise had been crucial at that moment.

For a split second, she'd been unable to comprehend his hesitation. Oh, she could understand why it would be a hard moment for him. She could tell he cared for Manny deeply, and treating a subdural hematoma was not without its dangers, even though trepanation and drainage often led to dramatic improvements in patients. It was a crude procedure, but it was effective. Even if they'd had time to bring Manny to a hospital in San Salvador, his treatment would have been much the same. The boy would most likely be on the mend within days.

At least that was one thing to be relieved about on a difficult day such as this. When everything else was going wrong.

Bryce had said he didn't want her pity. She thought about when he'd bandaged her ankle, and she'd told him about her heart defect. How she'd become known as Heart Defect Girl in school. She had never wanted to be seen just as someone with a heart defect. There was so much more to her than that. Just as Bryce probably didn't want to be seen as just an accident victim, a former surgeon with the best days of his career behind him.

She wondered if that's what he'd heard when she'd expressed her shock that he hadn't called her for help during such a difficult time in her life. It wasn't what she had meant. But then maybe he'd only heard what he was afraid of hearing.

If he had called, would they still be together now?

The question stopped her racing thoughts. Maybe that was the point. After the breakup, she'd felt so guilty about getting Bryce into trouble. She'd left him out of guilt. If he had called her, or if someone had told her that Bryce had been terribly injured in a life-altering car accident, she might have felt even guiltier because of his injuries. Perhaps even to the extent that she would have felt compelled to stay with him.

As much as she hated to admit it, maybe Bryce had been right not to contact her. He did know her, after all. He knew that if she found out about the accident, she would have come rushing to his side. But then Bryce would have had to deal with her presence while he was recovering, and she would have had to deal with her own feelings while also supporting him. It would have been very hard for both of them. If Bryce had reached out to her, then maybe they would still be together now. But it would be for all of the wrong reasons.

They'd both needed some space to grow in the past five years. He might not have been honest with her about everything, but the changes she saw in him were things he couldn't lie about. He was more easygoing, more carefree than he'd ever been when she had known him. Those changes were real. She thought again of their night in Juayua. Her response had been real.

She wondered who she would be today if she hadn't left Bryce all that time ago. As painful as the breakup had been, the last five years had helped her to know who she was in a way she could never have imagined. She wasn't the wild child she used to be, nor was she the straitlaced, buttoned-up Dr. Andover who did nothing but work, cook meals and then go to work again the next day.

She thought back to what she'd told Bryce on the bus. She'd tried to explain that for her, having adventures and taking risks were life-affirming. She'd meant it, from the bottom of her heart. But would she ever have realized that about herself if it hadn't been for that conversation with Bryce? She hadn't really thought about what it meant to her to be daring until she was confronted with the possibility of losing him again.

She would never have had that conversation with Bryce, or even with herself, if she hadn't come to El Salvador. For years, she'd told herself that she'd given up her daredevil personality because of what happened with Bryce. But she'd found that part of herself again because of him, too.

She'd done what she came here to do: she'd reconnected with her adventurous side. She had hoped she'd be able to do it without anyone getting hurt this time, but history, it seemed, was doomed to repeat itself.

At least this time, she knew what she needed to do next.

Bryce wasn't sure what it would be like to work with Cassie after their trip to Juayua, especially after he'd told her that he didn't see things working out between them. He was worried that their mutual discomfort would probably be distracting for both of them. But his concerns about working with her turned out to be unfounded. He barely ever saw her anymore. On the rare occasions when they did cross paths, she was excruciatingly polite. They kept their conversations short and professional. He missed the easy friendship that had built between them, but he didn't see any way for those times to return.

He considered asking Enrique if the two of them could be placed on opposite schedules, even though their awkward run-ins were already few and far between. But as he and Anna were talking together after a tough delivery, Anna mentioned how much she missed seeing Cassie during the day.

"What?" said Bryce. "Are you not seeing much of her, either?"

"She asked to be switched to night shift two weeks ago," Anna replied. "I guess maybe she needed a change. But it means we're not able to work together very often anymore. It's too bad. She's got such a reassuring way with patients."

It seemed there was no need to request a schedule change, as Cassie had beaten him to it. He didn't know if he should feel grateful that he wouldn't have to work the night shift or annoyed that Cassie had requested the change before he did. He supposed the important thing to focus on was that he didn't see Cassie very often at all.

It was a small consolation. He missed her terribly. He missed her banter, her laughter, their occasional squabbles over patients. He missed her, but it would have hurt more to see her.

Little Manny's recovery was going well. The biggest obstacle the medical team faced was trying to keep the boy still. He was curious as a squirrel, constantly being reminded that he couldn't run after the doctors to see what they were up to. Bryce tried to ease his restlessness by visiting frequently.

He was glad when a shipment of donated books and toys came in from San Salvador. He headed to the pediatric recovery tent, hoping that bringing a few of the new items to Manny would help to relieve his boredom. He was surprised to find the normally cheerful boy looking despondent.

"What's wrong?" Bryce asked as Manny sorted listlessly through the bundle Bryce had brought him.

"I miss Dr. Cassie," he said.

He felt a jolt through his stomach at Cassie's name.

"I understand," he said. "You don't get to see her as much anymore now that she's on night shift."

"No, I don't get to see her as much because she's *gone*," Manny said.

Bryce froze. "What do you mean *gone*?"

"She left a few days ago," said Manny,

mournfully. "She woke me up to say good-bye and said she wasn't sure when she was coming back." His teary eyes met Bryce's. "But she will come back, won't she?"

Bryce tried to conceal his shock. "I hope so," he said. And the moment he spoke the words aloud, he realized they were true.

For five years, he'd lived without Cassie in his life. And as difficult and painful as the last few weeks had been, he realized that nothing was more painful than the possibility that she might be gone from his life forever.

He had to find out if she were really gone. And if she was, then he wouldn't rest until he found a way to get her back.

CHAPTER TEN

BRYCE COULDN'T STAND another moment of uncertainty. He went directly to Enrique's tent. "Is it true?" he said, striding in.

"Hold on," said Enrique, who was wrapping up a conference call. He finished, and then turned to Bryce. "I could sit here and pretend to be naive, but I have a feeling I know what you're asking about. Or *whom* you're asking about."

"Is she really gone?"

"If you're talking about the best ob-gyn this camp has ever had, then yes, Dr. Andover is gone. She went back to New York. She said something about a job at her old hospital that sounded very interesting."

Bryce waved a hand dismissively. He didn't care about whether Cassie had her old job back. He cared that she was gone. "When did she leave?"

"A couple of days ago. She asked me to be discreet about it."

She'd been gone for days, and he hadn't noticed? His heart plummeted.

"In fact, I'll be blunt. She asked me specifically not to mention it to you when she left. But she did leave you a note." Enrique handed him an envelope.

A note. How appropriate. Would it always be notes with the two of them? He could see the outline of her writing from within the envelope. Clearly, she'd had much more to say this time than she had five years ago.

He opened the note.

Dear Bryce,

I wanted to leave you a better note this time. One that would force me to say everything our relationship deserves, no matter how hard it is to put the words down on paper. I used to think it was so important to live without fear, but thanks to you I know that it's even more important to live without regrets. And if I left El Salvador without you knowing how much our time together has meant to me…well, that would be a huge regret.

We've both talked about how we grew up in overprotective families. We probably both know, more than anyone, that sometimes you have to have some distance from the people you care for the most in order to grow. And so I'm leaving now, in order to give us both that distance and in the hope that we're both stronger, better people for it.

We've said some wonderful things about moving forward, but I guess Juayua showed us that we'd never be able to follow through. I have to admit that there were many, many times that I didn't want to follow through. Holding on to the past felt so good that I didn't really want to think about the future.

But we both need to move on, because we both deserve good futures. You, Bryce, deserve an amazing future. And I can't bear to stand in your way.
Cassie

He blinked back tears.

He'd messed up. He knew it. He'd been so worried about protecting his heart that he hadn't realized he was preventing himself from seeing what was right in front of him. He really was his parents' son. He'd grown up to be just as overprotective and obsessive as they were, except for him, his overprotectiveness was all directed toward his emotions. And now it had cost him everything. Unless there was a chance he could get it all back.

He knew, now, that he'd been foolish to ever think that he was just a thrill to her. She'd shown him that repeatedly. And if she also happened to be someone who needed excitement in her life...well, he'd learned that so did he. He'd never want to quell that adventurous side of her. It was an integral part of her...a part of her that he wanted in his life more than ever.

He folded the note into a small square and put it into his wallet. "I've got to find her."

Enrique sighed. "Why do I have a feeling I'm about to lose yet another one of my best doctors?"

"Just for a little while. I'll come back, I promise."

"Anything to help you figure out your love life," said Enrique. "Actually, it's fine. You've got more vacation days saved up than any of us. But...don't stay away too long, Bryce. We need you here. Come home soon. And bring her with you, if you can."

He felt that he'd have to be very, very lucky to come back with Cassie. Still, he had to try. He might not be able to find her in New York.

And then even if he did, she might not even want to see him.

It was just a risk he'd have to take.

It felt incredibly strange for Cassie to be back at Brooklyn General Hospital.

After just a couple months in El Salvador, it felt surreal to set foot in a New York hospital again. The rooms and hallways were immaculate and full of state-of-the-art equipment. The hospital was set up to take care of anything a patient needed, as well as some things they didn't. Cassie remembered all too well the requests many of her patients had made for specialty spa treatments as part of their birthing "packages." If a patient were wealthy enough, the hospital would provide anything that money could buy.

Despite all of the wealth on display, she was also struck by how impersonal the hospital was. She watched doctors and nurses reviewing charts and transporting patients, and she realized that she barely recognized any of the faces. When she'd worked here, she'd been so focused on her job that she hadn't had much time to form relationships with many of her team members. It was different at the medical camp, where everyone knew everyone else on sight. The small size of the camp made it easy to discern who did and didn't belong there. But here, even though she knew the entire layout of the hospital like the back of her hand, the people themselves were strangers. Even though she'd spent more time at work than at home over the past few years, these people didn't know her and she didn't know them.

But the impersonality of her surroundings was a small price to pay for the position and salary she'd just negotiated. Cassie had returned to her old hospital with a proposal. Brooklyn General, with its wealth of resources, was in an ideal position to form a liaison office with Medicine International. Doctors at Brooklyn General would be able to volunteer in El Salvador as well as other countries, and physicians from around the world would be able to consider Brooklyn General a home base to use for research, medical supplies and equipment. And Cassie would oversee it all.

The hospital administrators had been thrilled with the idea. It would make the hospital look good—a private hospital with a strong philanthropic outlook—and it would allow physicians to volunteer without having to leave their jobs as Cassie had. They were concerned, however, that overseeing the department would mean extensive amounts of travel to El Salvador and probably to many other countries, as well. Would Cassie be able to handle that?

She smiled and said that she thought she could make it work.

She walked out of the hospital's large double doors and took a deep breath, reveling in the warm sunshine. In a single afternoon, she'd set up a job that could provide all the adventure and excitement she would ever need.

The only thing to overshadow her happiness was the occasional thought of Bryce.

She knew she'd done the right thing by leaving, but that didn't make it any less painful.

Forward motion, she thought. She had left so that she and Bryce could move on. And for the past few days, she'd been doing exactly that. She had an exciting new job to look forward to, and as for her love life…maybe, someday, that would sort itself out. Until then, she was going keep trying to let go of the past and move forward.

To celebrate the good news about the job, she headed to her favorite coffee shop just across the street from the hospital.

She was standing in line to order when she felt a tap at her elbow. She looked down at a coffee cup. And the hand that was holding it belonged to Bryce.

"Black, with two sugars," he said.

"Bryce!" she cried. "What are you doing here?"

He gave her a lopsided smile. "Do you really have to ask? I got your note."

"But how did you know I was here?"

"A little social media detective work. Also it's a coffee shop. Any given coffee shop, on any given day, has a fifty-fifty chance of you being inside it. The odds were increased for this one, though, because I heard through a friend of a friend that you had a job interview at your old hospital today. It wasn't too hard to predict that you'd stop for coffee afterward."

Her eyes didn't leave his. Why had he come all this way?

She had a feeling it wasn't just to buy her a cup of coffee.

Although she did gratefully accept the cup. They headed outside into the sunshine.

As she sipped her coffee, he explained. "I did come because of your note. Because everything you said in it was right. And because it made me realize, finally, that you weren't leaving because you didn't care. You were willing to give up everything for both of our sakes, all over again. And I was so afraid of the past repeating itself that I couldn't even see the future that was unfolding right in front of me."

She smiled. "If I'd known this would be your reaction, I'd have left a better note five years ago."

He winced. "I should have called you after the accident. I should have known you would want to know. I was such an idiot."

She put a finger to his lips. "Neither of us made the brightest moves five years ago," she said.

"But I should have at least told you about it when you got to El Salvador," he said. "I guess I didn't because it felt as though you were looking at me in a way that you never used to. I wanted you to think that I was this brave person, someone who took risks and went on dangerous medical missions because I had courage. Not because I was someone who'd been through an accident, lost his chosen profession and didn't feel he needed to be as careful as he used to be."

"Oh, Bryce. You were so worried about what you lost. Didn't you notice what you'd built for yourself? Didn't you think I'd see that?"

"I wanted you to see that. I hoped you

would. But I was worried you'd compare me to who I used to be."

"Well, you were right about one thing."

"What's that?"

She smiled. "I *was* looking at you quite a bit."

He laughed.

"I can understand why you didn't tell me, but I wish you had," she said. "If only for the sake of being honest with each other."

"Honesty is always a good idea," he agreed.

"In the interest of total honesty, I should say that I'm glad you're here."

"Am I too late, though? It sounds like you've already got your old job back. If you're settling into your old life here, I'll understand."

She swatted his shoulder playfully. "My old job? Are you kidding me? That's not what I'm here for." She told him about the Medicine International liaison office she would be heading.

She carefully emphasized that the job would involve lots of travel, especially back and forth to Central American countries. In fact, there might even be a chance to build a strong relationship between the hospital and an El Salvador office.

"Wow," he said. "With all of that excitement in your life, I wonder if you might have room for someone who's just…ordinary."

She looked him square in the eye. "I don't know anyone who is *just* ordinary."

"But you do. You know me. And I've worked very hard to be okay with being ordinary."

"Bryce, you are *not* ordinary."

"I am, though. For years, I've been trying to be okay with the idea that I'm not gifted anymore. I'm not the person who handles all the challenging cases. I'm not the person who pulls off miracles in the operating room. I'm just a normal person who tries hard to be a good doctor. And it's taken me a long time to be okay with just being a normal person, because for so much of that time, I was competing with my past self. Instead of just trying to be me."

"And so you needed to get away from everyone else who was comparing you to your past self."

"Exactly. Because I had to accept that instead of being talented and admired and a star in the operating room, I was just plain old Bryce Hamlin. And being around other people who knew me in the old days made it so hard. Because if we're being honest, what's really so great about being plain old Bryce Hamlin?"

"For one thing, I'm in love with him."

The words had sprung from her lips, unbidden. She hadn't meant to say them. She hadn't planned it at all. But from the moment she'd seen Bryce at the coffee shop, she'd known it was true, even if she hadn't yet formed the words consciously in her mind.

She loved him. And no matter how he felt, she wanted him to know. She'd spent five years of her life without Bryce.

Five years, five months and twenty-three days, her brain supplied helpfully. The time that had passed, to the day, since she'd left that horrible note for him.

But she didn't want to spend another minute apart.

If writing the first note had been like tearing her heart out, writing the second had been like stomping it into the ground. But just like last time, she couldn't see any other way out of the situation.

Fortunately, Bryce could. She still wasn't sure what she'd written in that note to compel him to seek her out, but she supposed it didn't matter. He was here now. It was still hard to believe that he'd actually come all this way, that he'd found her. As they walked together, she slipped her arm into his. Partly to be companionable and partly to prove to herself that he was really there.

Her words still hung in the air between them. She'd taken a risk. But even though she didn't know what he would say, she didn't wish her words unsaid. Bryce had talked about the future. If they were going to have a future together, they'd need to be completely honest with each other, starting now. And the honest truth was, she loved him. And even if he didn't feel the same way, she needed him to know.

He took her hand, his brown eyes dark and wet. "You're in love with plain old Bryce Hamlin, huh?" His voice sounded rather dazed.

"Total honesty, remember?" She was still nervous, because he hadn't yet told her how he felt, but she gained confidence from knowing that her words reflected what she really, truly wanted to say to him. "You said that I've been looking at you in a different way. And maybe you're right. But it has nothing to do with the fact that you were riding a motorcycle, or negotiating with gang leaders, or going on midnight rides through the mountains to deliver vaccines. It never had anything to do with that.

"I fell in love with your kindness, Bryce. I fell in love with the look on your face when you hand a baby to a new mother. I fell in love with your determination to protect everyone in your care. And none of that has anything to do with you being a gifted surgeon. It has to do with you being a committed doctor and a compassionate human. That's who plain old Bryce is."

"Wow," said Bryce. "He sounds like a pretty swell guy."

"I think so. When he's not being a complete lunkhead."

"This ordinary Bryce...he sounds like he has a lot of people depending on him."

"Oh, yes. There are colleagues back in El Salvador who are counting on him to return as soon as possible. There are patients who need his help. And there's a ten-year-old boy whose heart is aching for him to return."

"Well—" he took the arm that was entwined with hers and pulled her close to him "—it sounds like plain old Bryce has a pretty amazing life. Awesome job, great friends and colleagues, and...someone who loves him." He put his arms around her, touched his forehead to hers. "And he loves her right back."

He kissed her then, his lips demanding that her mouth open, and she yielded readily to the touch of his mouth on hers. For a moment, she was completely lost, the sensation of his kiss invading her senses. And there again was that cedar spice smell, tingling at her nose.

Suddenly, she had an idea. She wasn't sure how Bryce would react but...*total honesty*, she thought.

"Wait," she said, pulling away from him. She got down on one knee, still holding his hand in hers. His eyes widened. She definitely hadn't planned on doing this today, but now that they were here, she knew it felt right. Five years ago, Bryce had wanted to propose to her, but he'd been rejected before he even got the chance. She wasn't going to put him through that again. At that time, she'd led him to believe that she wasn't serious about their relationship. She wanted him to know, here and now, that she was ready for commitment.

As she took his hand and knelt before him, a flutter of nerves overtook her stomach. *Damn, this really is nerve-racking. What if it's not the right time? What if he says no? No wonder it's hard for so many men to get up the nerve to do this.*

Anxiety washed over her. She could feel Bryce's hand shake a little, but she held it steady in hers. If there was ever a time to jump in with both feet, this was it.

"I want to ask you something."

"Cassie."

"Just let me finish. I want to do this properly. Five years ago, you were going to put your heart on the line for me. And now I'm going to put mine on the line for you."

"Cassie."

"I don't have a ring, or anything. But we can—"

"Would you look at your hand?"

She looked at her hand, the one he was holding. The copper spark of the motorcycle ignition ring winked back from her from where it rested around her ring finger. Her mind seemed to be working very slowly. She kept looking back and forth from his face to her hand, trying to absorb what had just happened. Then she stood up with a start.

Finally, she managed to croak out a question. "How long have I been wearing this?"

"I'm not exactly sure, but I think it was somewhere around the words *total honesty.*"

"That long? I can't believe I didn't notice!"

His smile went from ear to ear. "Then it must feel pretty natural for you to wear it."

She was still staring at the ring in amazement. He put both arms around her. She leaned into him and he nuzzled her hair.

"If our goal is to be totally honest, then

I want to start by being honest about how I feel." He tilted her chin up toward his. "I love you, Cassie. I love everything about you, but most of all, I love your adventurous side. I love the part of you that pushes me past my limits. I don't know how I've managed to get through the last five years of my life without you, and I don't want to waste another minute anywhere other than by your side. I love you, and now that I've finally got you back, I'm going to hold on to you with both hands."

He kissed her deeply, but after a moment she had to break away. She was smiling too hard to hold his kiss. There were tears in her eyes, which he brushed away. "Happy tears, I hope?" he said.

"You know they are."

He kissed her again. "Now, I don't want to be presumptuous. But given that you got down on one knee just a moment ago…can I assume the answer is yes?"

"That would be a safe assumption."

He buried his nose in her hair again. "We can get you a real engagement ring. I've been holding on to this as a good luck charm. I just used it because I happened to have it handy. The moment I saw you, I knew I had to take the chance. We'll head to a jewelry store tomorrow and you can pick out something beautiful."

"Oh, no," she said. "This one is perfect. It's already beautiful. Besides, we don't have time to go ring shopping. We'll need to get started on wedding planning soon if we want to get married before we head back to El Salvador."

The smile on his face told her everything she needed to know about his desire for a quick wedding. "It sounds like a plain old New York City Hall wedding might be in order for plain old Bryce Hamlin."

She kissed him. "Sounds perfect."

"Are you sure that's okay? You don't want a big wedding?"

She poked him in the side. "I want a fast wedding. I've spent the past five years not being married to you, and I don't think I can take it for another minute longer than I absolutely have to. Besides, people are waiting for us in El Salvador."

"My poor motorcycle. At least it gets a chance to live on with us."

"It's the perfect ring. It tells our story. I wouldn't want anything else. Unless you want to keep it for luck?"

"It's brought me all the luck I need," he

said. And they were quiet for quite some time after that.

When they did stop kissing, Cassie wanted to know how Bryce had had the courage to slip the ring on her finger. "How did you know I'd say yes?"

"I didn't! I knew that it might all end in disaster. But I had to take the risk. I remembered what you said about living rather than just surviving. I wanted to live, so I decided to put the ring on your finger and see what happened. I knew that even if you didn't say yes, it was the right thing to do."

"How come?"

He snuggled closer to her. "Because I've realized that bravery has nothing to do with the danger you're facing and everything to do with what's in your own heart."

She wrapped her arms around him and considered her own heart. Broken and repaired, a hundred times over. But for all the trouble her heart had caused her, it was hers, and it was the kind of heart that showed who she was. Maybe her heart hadn't started life in the strongest shape, but with enough love and care, it had healed. And that made sense to her. Learning to love, she knew now, wasn't about guarding your heart or trying desperately to keep it from getting broken.

Love wasn't about protecting your heart from getting hurt. It was about trusting that it would heal when it did.

* * * * *

If you enjoyed this story, check out this other great read from Julie Danvers

From Hawaii to Forever

Available now!